Twenty-Eight
Days

Twenty-Eight Days

NINA TRACY

URBAN BOOKS
http://www.urbanbooks.net

This is a work of fiction. Any references or similarities to actual events, real people, living or dead, or to real locales are intended to give the novel a sense of reality. Any similarity in other names, characters, places, and incidents is entirely coincidental.

URBAN SOUL is published by

Urban Books
1199 Straight Path
West Babylon, NY 11704

ISBN-13: 978-1-59983-062-9
ISBN-10: 1-59983-062-0

First Printing: June 2008

10 9 8 7 6 5 4 3 2 1

Printed in the United States of America

Chronic Antidote

*Did you feel the slight tremble as you proceeded to
  come inside*
*Or the meager quiver I produced as your hand
  mildly grazed my thigh*
*Could you tell I wanted to scream but was afraid
  someone would hear*
*Or that you would err the emotion as anguish if I
  dared to shed a tear*
*How did you know just what to do to make me feel
  that way*
*The fruition you entrusted me with left me speech-
  less without an utterance to say*
*I'm reliving the copulation every instant even now
  as my hand tremors to write*
*As I close my eyes and dream of being held again in
  your clutches tonight*

*I'm appreciative of the appetizing taste but am
  longing for a plentiful bite*
*Of the tantalizing delicacy that only you can pre-
  pare just right*
*I feel like a peasant, a beggar, a person indulging
  in greed*
*Unable to distinguish impulsive wants from life's
  required needs*

*I want so badly to place upon myself a degree of
    disgrace and shame
But the thought of you sends my heart pounding,
    causing my emotions to become untamed
Now I find myself with the same tactility as I had
    before
Too naïve to have realized that this ailing passion
    would have such an addictive cure*

Prologue

Lonely?

I must admit to having been somewhat taken back by the question posed to me by the young tenderoni. "Are you desperately lonely?" he had asked a few minutes after we had pulled up in front of his dwelling, after having shared an intimate spell together and then grabbing a fast-food combo. The truck door was open, and his legs dangled out. He sipped on the vanilla milk shake that had come with his meal as he waited on my reply.

Hmm, well, let me think. First of all, I was kicking myself for taking too damn long to respond, but at the same time I was saying to myself, *What do you think, fool?*

Here I was sitting my pushing thirty-year-old ass across from what could very well be a replica of my step son, plus nine years. The fact that I was a very successful executive at a Fortune 500 company, who owned a very nice home in the suburbs, plus three investment properties, and was the mother of two, who happened to still look good, didn't seem to matter. Here I sat, somewhat ashamed but halfway flattered by the "I'm about to turn twenty-one" black man sitting next to me, about to get out of my truck.

Why didn't I just pull up in front of the house, slow down, and make his ass jump out? I questioned myself. No, I just had to sit here and make small talk with someone who couldn't hold an intelligent conversation on my level if his life depended on it. There he sat, only confirming my conclusion, wearing a white T- shirt halfway to his knees, under an army camouflage down coat. He also wore an oversized New York Yankees baseball hat and jeans that had to be two sizes too big, with no belt at that. His Timberland boots were unlaced.

The answer to his question, to me, was clear. As a matter of fact, it was written all over my face, or at least I thought it was. But just in case he was having a problem interpreting the writing on the wall, I tilted my head, smacked my lips, and twisted them to the side. Certainly the answer was now clear. *Fool, why else would I be sitting here with your young ass, picking you up and dropping you back off in my truck in front of your momma's house because you don't have a car yet, and embarrassed that all of these folks around your hood are looking at me like I done robbed the cradle?*

If I wasn't desperately lonely before, I sure the fuck was now! I wanted to be pissed at him for asking me that stupid-ass question. How dare he make me face the reality that I had been trying to escape from ever since my divorce! Ever since my husband had left me for another woman: a younger woman. Was this some subconscious payback? If it was, to whom was the debt owed? Because as far as I could tell, I was the only one this transaction was having a negative effect on.

Paying my gestures no attention whatsoever, he sipped on his shake and posed the question once again. "Are you desperately lonely?"

As I pondered his question, I wanted to get my back straight, like I was indignant that he had even fixed his pouty lips to ask a grown-ass woman such as myself that question, but instead, I erased that fucked-up look from my face, changed my disposition to one more my age, and gave a polite, ladylike verbal response.

"I keep myself way too busy for that."

Bullshit, bullshit, bullshit. I wanted to beat my fist on the steering wheel. The truth was, I had allowed myself to go out like this, with this young boy who had just barely turned in his high school graduation cap for the fitted cap he was now wearing on his head, and all for a little stroking and a few flattering words from the mouth of a babe. Thank God I hadn't actually fucked him . . . yet. He was supposed to be my escape, just a mini vacation from reality. And just when I thought I had escaped reality's bite, the little tyke brought up another good question. And this time the little nitwit went straight for the jugular. "Why hasn't anybody snatched you up?"

Yeah, why hadn't anybody snatched me up? And why had my ex-husband thrown me away?

Once again, I maintained my composure. Through my open leather coat, I pulled down the little crop top I had thrown on especially for my outing with him, thinking it would make me look and feel like I belonged with the company I was keeping. Instead, it made me feel like something I was not. Ironically, though, hadn't that been the entire purpose? But I didn't like the way I was feeling; like a girl trapped in a woman's body. I looked over at him and very kindly said, "Honey, close the door."

He lifted his legs, which had been dangling outside, into the truck as he continued to suck on his milk shake. Right when he went to grab the truck door to pull it closed, I said, "No, sweetie." I patted him on his knee. "Get out first, and then close the door."

He had this puzzled look on his face, unable to speak because his mouth was filled with the frozen dairy product. I shooed him along by waving my hand, scooting him right on out of my vehicle. He watched my smoke as I skidded off.

Through the rearview mirror, I saw where I had left him standing there, holding his head, with a frozen headache from the shake rushing to his brain. I then looked at myself in the mirror. Me, I had a frozen heart. I couldn't have cared less about the feelings of that young lad, whom I would never see again, or about any other man's feelings for that matter. It was now all about me!

It was at that moment that I decided that I needed to make a change in my life, and fast. What had I been thinking when I hooked up with that young'n? Was I really that desperate and lonely that I thought he could bring something out in me that I knew was buried deep inside? Did I think he could bring out that young, rambunctious chick inside of me who I had sealed up and traded in for a life of marriage and having babies?

I had it all wrong. I was looking toward the wrong source to bring out that chick that had been shackled beneath my womanly skin through eight years of marriage that ended in failure. I should have been looking toward my inner self. After all, I was to blame for her own imprisonment in the first place, so I needed to be the one who enabled her to break free.

There was so much that the person inside of me needed to do that she had never been able to do, and now here I was, getting older with the realization that the crazy shit I used to do with my girlfriends and get away with must come to an end. That scared me, because on my upcoming birthday, I would be putting an end to something that had never even gotten a chance to begin.

I couldn't let the opportunity to give birth to the sexual creature inside of me slip away in a matter of days. I couldn't live my life vicariously through erotic books and movies. I needed to experience some things for myself.

As if I was an author who had just gotten a brilliant story line for a book, I pulled my truck over and dug out a piece of paper and pen from my glove box. I proceeded to write down every single sexual fantasy that I had ever longed to experience. I then set what some might see as an unattainable goal; I planned to experience every last one of those fantasies.

I pulled out my little planner from my purse. In a little over a month, on February 1, I would be celebrating my twenty-eighth birthday. I had never been a genius in math, but the calculation was simple. I had a list of fantasies that I had to experience, and I had a short period of time to do them. Could I, one woman, accomplish such a task in so little time? Hmm, I'm not sure, but I'm going to have a hell of a time finding out. Won't you join me for the ride . . . ?

Chapter One

The Sex Diva

Twenty-eight days. A slow smile crept across my face, and a warm sensation began at my thighs and warmed my entire being. It was sheer pleasure I felt when I look back at the month of February. The shortest month of twelve, but by far the most pleasurable I had had in all my years on this earth.

It was ironic to me that the same month of my twenty-eighth birthday, I made a promise to myself to explore every sexual fantasy I had ever imagined, and then some. I liked to think of it as a coming-of-age, a mini revolution of my very own, and the month that I totally rebelled, breaking every sexual taboo that had been imprinted in my little head from birth.

Little girls are raised to be gentle, ladylike, and pure. Mothers raise their daughters to be the kind of woman a man would bring home to Momma, not the bad girl that is always willing and ready to receive him. Well, I listened closely to what Momma had to say. I followed the rules. Unfortunately, life ended up dealing me a shitty hand when it came to men and relationships. I played the role a woman was supposed to play. I ended up crapping out several times. So, needless to say, I don't give a damn about rules. And it wasn't until I started to fuck the rules, literally, that my life got a whole lot more interesting.

In order for you to understand with an open mind where I am at in my life now, you have to understand where I came from. So let me start with that rat bastard ex-husband of mine.

After my divorce, I was beyond devastated. I'd look at myself in the mirror and try to see if, in the reflection, I could figure out where I had gone wrong. I had honestly thought that I was doing everything right to keep a tight grip on my man and our precious relationship.

I gave him two beautiful and intelligent children. I held down my duties by nursing them, nurturing them, teaching them, feeding them, and making sure they had nice clean clothes to wear, everything a good mother should do. Hell, I was the goddamn village!

When a man painted a picture of the type of woman whom he wanted to settle down with and raise his children, I made it a point to be that woman. I made sure that I was every stroke of the paintbrush. Every crevice on the canvas. The hell with the *Mona Lisa*, I was a living portrait, if I don't say so myself . . . at least I thought I was, which takes me back to the rat bastard and his leaving me for another woman. I hope you don't mind me referring to him as such, but after all of the hurt and pain he caused me, I can't even stand to put his name on my lips. And I get sick just thinking about all the other parts of him that I used to put my lips on.

I had stood by my man just like those dumb-ass country and western songs tell women they are supposed to do. I cooked, cleaned, and carpooled. When I suspected him of cheating, I turned the other cheek, waiting and relying on proof positive instead of my women's intuition. I was a model mother and wife. The problem was, that was all I was . . . a model. I was no different than those plastic dummies people see in department store windows, posing pretty, but dead inside. I was consumed with expectations. I got caught up in making sure I fulfilled the expectations that society had placed on me concerning who I was and what I was supposed to be. Don't get me wrong. I loved being a momma to my two lovely children. I loved my husband. But, hell, a bitch wanted to live!

Eventually, the same way those plastic dummies in the store go unnoticed by customers, I started to go unnoticed by my man. Instead of growing to appreciate me more for the things I was doing to hold the household and family down, he grew to expect the supernatural out of this superwoman I had made myself out to be. I became commonplace, just another fixture in our home, in our marriage, in our life. Even after a while, Lois Lane didn't get excited when she saw Superman fly. Hell, she had grown to expect the mutherfucker to fly, so it no longer excited her. After a while, he just became a nigga who could fly. That pretty much describes how my husband started to see me.

Fuck that! I wanted my man to worship me, to take me outside in the rain and make me call out his name. To take me to the top floor of the tallest downtown building, in a glass elevator, and then eat me out all the way down to the ground floor. To take me to the nasty places I saw on HBO's *Real Sex* and do naughty things to me. I wanted him to whip his "dude" out and let me go down on him while driving down the highway . . . in broad daylight . . . even at a red light where the people in the truck stopped next to us could watch my every move. I had a craving to make my fantasies become his and my dirty little secret that we would take to our graves. After all, it was supposed to be until death do us part, and I wanted to give the term a whole other meaning.

I was versatile, but this was a hidden quality I guess I never really did feel comfortable revealing to my husband. He just didn't seem like he could appreciate it in me. He had his vision of what a wife and mother was supposed to be and never thought outside of that box he had drawn and placed me in . . . locking it and throwing away the key for eight long years.

I could have easily played a dual role as housewife slash hooker. I would have loved to be my husband's whore. The problem with that was that I felt trapped inside of the stereotypes that trick women into acting as if the only purpose of the act of sex is to create another life. Sex is much more than that. Granted, I would never in a million years change the hand I was dealt when it came to reproduction and God using my womb to bear the two blessings in my life, but if I had to do it all over again, I would definitely spice up the act in which my little dependents were conceived.

I do not regret that the urge to express the full realm of my sexuality came upon me too little, too late in my life. Maybe just snatching off my cape, completely losing myself, and having no inhibitions could have saved my marriage. But on the same token, perhaps my newfound sexuality wasn't intended to be expressed with my then husband. After all, we were total opposites from the start. I was always the more outgoing one, allowing him to tone me down so that I could be the woman he wanted me to be. That woman he saw as wifey . . . as baby momma. So guess what? It was his loss.

I do regret that I didn't go on this journey of self-indulgence before I settled down into a marriage. Because maybe deep down inside, I was only hurting myself by keeping locked up that chick who desperately wanted to break through the skin of the woman everybody saw on the outside.

I guess, looking on the bright side, baby, I'm a grown-ass, fully functioning, and independent woman. Sexy as hell; smart as fuck; still a good mammy, who is able to whip up a mouthwatering meal, kick it with the kids, and never let him (wherever he is and whenever he finds me) forget he's a man.

I am okay with the fact that I like to fuck. Why should it be so taboo for a woman to voice and be comfortable with the fact that she enjoys the intensity and stimulation of sexual acts? I enjoy sucking dick, taking it from the back like a big girl, and even participating in an orgy or two. And another female in the mix every now and then for some variety won't hurt my feelings at all. But when it comes to adding another pussy into the mix with my dick, I do have a control problem with those types of things. I like to say who, when, and how. But then again, that could just be the dominatrix in me.

I don't feel guilty at all about loving to have good,

exciting, clean, protected sex. I don't feel any woman should. Why should men be the only ones allowed to voice such pleasures? Why should men have this license to fuck that doesn't have any restrictions? And I think that's the problem with a lot of relationships. Women allow themselves to be confined to one role and one role only. They become afraid to live outside of the box—the box society, mostly controlled by men, has confined them to. We end up becoming children in grown-up bodies. I should know. I used to be one of those women.

My role as a married woman was similar to that of the children who were produced in the marriage. It was considered better that I be seen rather than heard. I guess some men take that text in the New Testament, 1 Timothy, 2:11–13, to heart. ("Let the woman learn in silence with all subjection. But I suffer not a woman to teach, nor to usurp authority over the man, but to be in silence. For Adam was first formed, then Eve.")

My marriage ended up suffocating my identity and left my self-esteem in the dust. Having married just a couple years out of high school to escape the turmoil in my mother's home, I can admit to leaving one hell only to escape to another. At the tender age of twenty-one, I married a replica of my father, a well-educated brother, well spoken, condescending as hell, and about as emotionless as a rock. I will admit to being intrigued by my ex's pro-black preachings and teaching, and his confident swagger. I was impressed that this young single father of two sons, Kaheem and Omari, was holding it down by raising his children in the home that he alone had made for them. Of course, I had to give his mother credit for that. She had taught her baby well in the area of parenting.

I was absolutely starstruck at the fact that he owned fatherhood in a way I could never understand. Having been brought up in a family full of women, my only experience with daddies was seeing them come and go. They'd come, and for a while, everything would be good. Then, as soon as the woman would pop up pregnant, the arguments started. Like clockwork, before the baby was even walking, there he'd go. I never did understand why a baby's first word was always "Da-da" when that was the person they connected with the least, if at all.

This pattern of coming and going was repeated from my momma to my aunties, so I never had any high expectation of men once they became dads. I just prepared myself for either not having babies at all or putting myself in a position to do it on my own. That was until I met Rahmel, my ex, a young single father who had fought for the right to raise his children. He couldn't care less that their mother was running the streets as long as the judge saw to it that he was their custodial parent. The rat bastard might not have put succeeding in marriage high on his list of priorities, but the act of parenting was definitely placed on a pedestal by him. I mean, he absolutely cherished his little boys with all of his heart. I remembered seeing him interact with his young sons and thinking, Now this is a real man.

I had never seen a man, black or white, take such pride and pleasure in fighting to be the sole caregiver of his children. I wanted to be a part of that. Looking back, I think watching how he raised his children made me want him to raise me. Maybe be that father to me that I never had in my own life. Just another trap we women set for ourselves: the desire to find Daddy in another man. Nonetheless, I couldn't wait for this man to take me up under his wing.

As soon as I gained the confidence to leave my momma's house, I was hell-bent on moving into Rahmel's tiny, roach-infested apartment in the hood. As long as I was with him, nothing else even mattered. Yeah, Lauryn Hill definitely had that shit right when she and D'Angelo did that song.

Life in Mother's home had been rough, though. I saw a lot of shit go down that no child should ever see from a stranger, let alone their mammy. Momma went from being a teenage mother to a midlife junkie, and being the oldest of three meant I was the one cleaning up all my mother's junkie messes.

I can still remember her dragging me from one medical center to another on a stolen welfare insurance card, trying her best to cop some prescription narcotics. On more than one occasion, she even used me as bait, telling me that there would be no Christmas in our home if I didn't get on that table and give the performance of a lifetime so she could persuade the doctor to prescribe me some medicine for her to sell. Needless to say, I got an Academy Award.

Now that I think about it, Momma's coaching me to give the appearance of being one step away from my deathbed may have led to a tiny piece of my success. In high school I excelled in theater, and my reenactment of *For Colored Girls Who Have Considered Suicide When the Rainbow Is Enuf* by Ntozake Shange was my ticket to winning the Miss Black Teen pageant. And the pageant was how I met Rahmel.

We were both speakers at a community center's antidrug rally. The moment I saw him and heard him speak, that was all she wrote. The rest was history, as they say. I guess Momma's pitiful displays of motherhood were worth something.

My mother was shady, and as much as I wanted to leave, it took months for me to get the courage to go. Looking my little brother and sister in the eyes and walking out the door, knowing that I was throwing them to the wolves, were the hardest things I've ever had to do.

I can remember my mother following me from room to room, with a laundry list of reasons why I shouldn't go. Hot on Momma's heels was my eleven-year-old sister, Kayla, and nine-year-old brother, Isaiah, tearfully begging, "Please, Sissy, don't go! Mommy, tell her you're going to do better. Tell her!"

I had endured my mother's home far too long for the sake of them. I had to go. I was confident I had given them the tools they needed to survive, and if any shit hit the fan, I was only a phone call away. But for right now, as long as I was with Mel, as I called Rahmel, nothing else even mattered.

During the first couple of years, Rahmel, the children, and I struggled. But as long as we were together in the struggle, I was a happy camper. I can remember standing at the altar, with a perfect white summer dress I had gotten off the clearance rack at an outlet store, a pair of white shoes I borrowed from Mel's sister, and a fresh beauty school hairdo. Rahmel was dressed in traditional African garb that did nothing to complement my ensemble, but I didn't give a damn. We stood at that altar with his two sons, little

Kaheem and Omari. His mother was present also, and, of course, the pastor.

I meant every word I said when I promised to love, honor, and obey until death do us part. I couldn't wait to go off and start our little family.

As soon as I posted up in Rahmel's tiny two-bedroom apartment, I set about the business of making it into a home. My first order of business was to get rid of the roaches. I cleaned out every cupboard and bombed that apartment like it was under attack. We camped out at my mother-in-law's until the smoke had cleared, and two days later, I came in loaded for bear.

With an arsenal of Mr. Clean and bleach, I swept through that apartment like a tornado. It wasn't hard to do. All he had was a mattress on the floor, a couple boatloads of books, and piles of clothes folded neatly along the walls. Every penny I earned from the tiny day care I worked in went to furnishing our home. I got so savvy in my shopping that I had the kind old ladies at the local thrift store gave me a ring whenever a worthy piece of furniture was brought into the store. It wasn't long before I had our tiny apartment looking like one of the designer showcase rooms I had seen in a magazine. I had copied the picture almost to a tee. We didn't have much, but what we lacked in material things, I made up for with plenty of TLC.

I have plenty of fond memories from the early years in our marriage. I can remember the first time we walked little Kaheem, Rahmel's oldest boy, to the bus stop for his first day of school. He was too short to even reach the first step, and my heart swelled when I saw the tears in Rahmel's eyes as he lifted Kaheem onto the bus and told him to be brave, even though Daddy was not being a big boy at the moment, unlike him.

Rahmel and I would catch the bus down to the small college we both attended and meet each other in the cafeteria in between classes to shoot the breeze. One afternoon, when a conversation about sex led from a simple "what if" to an all-out mission, we snuck into the ladies' restroom at school and did the damn thing in the handicapped stall.

I can remember the rush I got from doing something I wasn't supposed to do. I loved those very rare occasions when we pushed the envelope sexually. For a split second, I felt like we were on the brink of igniting our sex life into a flame. But as the years progressed and I started to have babies of my own, that rush I felt in college seemed to move further and further from my reach.

Miles was born as we entered our third year of marriage, and Ariel followed right behind him. No sooner had I taken my titty from Miles's little lips and lit his first birthday candles than I discovered I was pregnant once again.

Motherhood was my calling, and I owned it with all my might. I was determined to be the best I could be. They say hindsight is twenty-twenty, and in my mind's eye, what was happening around me was crystal clear. While I was focused on raising my four children, Rahmel was slipping from my grasp.

I think somewhere in all the transitions from being a poor, young family to moving on up to middle-class citizens, I may have become more of a mother than a wife. While I was once a part of college life, social events, and the pro-black rallies, I had become an occasional attendee, preferring to stay at home and do the momma thing. I guess I just assumed that the tingle I had in college would resurface once the kids got a little bit older. You know what they say about assumptions; well, I ended up looking like the ass when my cookie started to crumble.

The seven-year itch hit our marriage hard and fast. Rahmel had always been a distant brother, quiet and to himself. He was a man of few words. Spoke more with his eyes and gentle touch, but toward the end, he became a complete stranger to me. To the children, though, he was still just Daddy.

If my husband had proved nothing else to me in our marriage, it was that he was a damn good dad. Then, one day, I realized that I, and even the kids, to a certain degree, was being replaced by the damn computer. In a desperate state, I remember confiding to my mother about the distance that had formed in my household, not that she was an expert on keeping a man or anything, but for once I took the advice my mother had offered me.

I dropped the kids off with her one day after they got out of school, and I rushed home and put on some skimpy lingerie and made my way to Rahmel's home office, where he had spent most of the day. I wrapped my arms around him and placed soft kisses on his neck. I looked up at the computer screen, and noticing that he was engaged only in a game of online chess, I continued my seduction, only to be cut off midstream.

"Gimme ten minutes, Nina. I can't log off in the middle of the game."

Needless to say, my mouth dropped. I mean, my

entire intention behind going in there was to drop my
mouth, but onto his dick, not the fucking floor. I
looked down at myself to make sure that Vickie's
secret was out. All looked fine, but yet this nigga was
choosing a computerized game of chess over his
wife.

I tried my best to be a good sport and posted up on
the futon that sat behind his desk. I lay there in an attempt to strike my best "come get 'em, tiger" pose.
Ten minutes turned into thirty, and then thirty into an
hour. At an hour and a half, a bitch finally took the
hint, leaving the room, with my panties in a bunch.

Before I could make heads or tails out of what was
happening to my life, I happened upon Rahmel's
password to his e-mail account, which he had jotted
down in his address book. Come on now. I am a
woman. Despite my feelings of wanting to stand by
my man . . . blah, blah, blah . . . my intuition was as
keen as ever. I'll admit to being ill prepared for the
string of e-mails that he had both sent and received
from his "soul mate." E-mails that consisted of
everything from love poems to elaborate plans to
take a trip together to the motherland. He was planning an entire future with this woman that did not in-
clude me.

I found one particular poem that made me feel as
though someone had stuck their hand down my
throat and ripped my guts out. Not because it was so
intimate, but because it was familiar. It was a poem I
had written Rahmel inside of a card back when we
first started dating. I was touched that he had saved
it and remembered, but I couldn't believe that he had
sent it to her. I wasn't mistaken as I read it, for I knew
the poem by heart:

"For Lovers Only"

when i look into your eyes
let me tell you what i see:
how my life would be different
if you belonged to me;

your kind smile;
your soft, gentle touch;
i guess that's what makes me want you so
much.

but what if you were mine?
then would it be another i desire
to respond to my womanly cries
and to adore me until i tire?

a warm embrace;
a pliant kiss;
i guess these are the things i'm afraid i'll miss.

so let's share this moment
as we have all the others.
the want for devotion i'll ignore
and concentrate only on being lovers.

meanwhile, every second, every minute, and
every hour of time
i'll be fascinated by the fantasy of you being mine.

My tears dripped onto the keyboard as I moved the
cursor about to open other e-mails. I stumbled upon
some pictures of her that she had e-mailed him.
Seeing the bitch didn't make the pill any easier to

swallow. It looked like she had stepped right out of the pages of some fucking Egyptian fable and into my husband's heart. This bitch was queen mother earth wrapped in kente cloth, with long, flowing dreadlocks and cocoa skin. Her petite frame was much different from my healthy curves. She looked as if a little dick would break her in two. But never mind me; I'm just hatin', of course. To make it even worse, I had met her before. I had been introduced to her as Rahmel's wife, so the bitch knew she was creeping with somebody else's husband.

So, loaded with knowledge of the electronic affair that was transpiring, I did the only thing I could given my situation. I swallowed my pride and confronted the rat bastard. That was when I learned that their relationship had gone far beyond just the realm of cyberspace. The two had been physically intimate.

I told him I was prepared to forgive provided we take certain steps to secure our marriage and that he never make contact with nubianme08@aol.com again. As it turned out, and in the exact words of my ex-husband, my "finding out was just the out I needed to push on with my life and renew myself." What the hell kind of psychobabble was this?

I struggled to hold on to my marriage and family, the only semblance of a normal (for whatever that word is worth) family that I'd ever experienced. Rahmel, on the other hand, had been through with our relationship for months, maybe even years, before the papers were signed that severed our marital contract, the one we had entered into when we mouthed before a man of the cloth that we would be committed to each other until death do us part. Well,

I guess you could say our love for each other had died. Does that type of death count?

Whether we still loved each other or not, or were in love with each other, the divorce left me a pretty mess. I had two kids, a mortgage, a car note, and banged-up self-esteem. How dare that bastard fall out of love with me? Who gave him that right? I was the one who wore the goddamn cape in this relationship. But I guess I was the one who had given him permission to mold me into just the woman he wanted me to be, only for him to throw me away like three-day-old milk ('cause y'all know we gon' drink that shit for at least two more days after the expiration date). I was the only one who had the right to fall out of love. Not him . . . me! Yeah, I was on some Kelis, the first chick to scream on a track, "I hate you so much right now" shit.

I left my mother's house to escape the burdens of being the oldest child and the one who had to pick up the pieces whenever Momma fell off the proverbial wagon. During my years with Rahmel, I began to distance myself from my friends and family, focusing only on my life with him and our young family.

I changed my wardrobe to please my husband, because in his opinion, a beautiful woman didn't need eye-catching attire in order to be admired unless, of course, she was trying to seduce, and as a wife, that was not my place. He preferred me without make-up or any other artificial extras, like acrylic nails or a hair weave, unless it happened to be braids, of course. I understand now that it was my naivete that led me to make such drastic changes in order to please a man. I even gave up Christmas, my favorite holiday of the year, because Mel believed it was a "strictly commercial holiday." Hell, it might have been, but the memories of my momma and me scraping together all we could so that Christmas could be possible were some of the fondest memories I had of our relationship.

For quite some time after the divorce, my insecurities kept me from dating. And when I did date, it wasn't usually the pick of the litter, but the runt instead, the one that was left over. After all, who was I to deserve the best? Why would the best want me? Who would want me, period? I had been created to fit another man, and I felt that it was written all over me, and who would want a woman with another man's dick print left on her? Besides, I had been spoiled twice with two young children. Who would want to deal with that? is what I asked myself time and again. So pretty soon, my focus became work and kids. Day in and day out, I built this façade around me, trying to let people know that a man didn't make or break me. I was going to keep it moving. One passenger getting off didn't stop my train.

I was on a mission to redeem myself before those who looked upon me with a message in their eyes that said, "Poor, li'l thing. What is she gonna do now?" I was hell-bent on not ending up like my sorry-assed mother, who, for as long as I could remember, had been more worried about partying and men than she had been about her own children. I was determined to make my way for me and my shorties, so I plunged into the world of advertising with a vengeance, advertising myself that is, oh yeah, and pursuing a career in advertising as well. But my main focus was getting myself together on the inside as well as the outside.

I worked my butt off in the gym, making sure I was

tight to death in appearance. And to prove that I was just as original as the spoon-fed college graduates who walked through the door as if their diploma had earned them a red carpet or something, I began to further my own education.

I worked a full-time job, and when the day was over, I came home to the kids, homework, and just the daily grind itself, only to go to bed at night and wake up to do it all over again the next day. All the things that I thought I was doing to better myself and keep up the image I was portraying were, in actuality, beginning to play out like a hamster running for dear life on a wheel that was leading to the Land of No-fuckin'-where.

I made attempts to keep the relationship with my stepsons as solid as the one I had with Ariel and Miles. The fucked-up thing about stepkids is if you choose to step up and own that relationship in the way in which I had done with mine but are no longer in a relationship with their biological parent, then you don't really understand that you don't "own" anything at all until you're told in no uncertain terms that you have no rights whatsoever.

I was able to pick up Kaheem and Omari on a few occasions, and we managed to have a pretty good time despite the obvious. Being that the boys were thirteen and twelve, they weren't as oblivious to the root cause of the breakup as Miles and Ariel. My invisible umbilical cord was stripped when we tripped into a conversation about what really went down that caused the breakup of Mel and me. I had always maintained an open-door policy, insisting that no topic was off limits, and therefore, I was fair game when the topic of our divorce came up.

Kaheem looked me in the eye and said, with no hesitation, "You and Dad didn't really just stop loving each other, huh, Ma?"

"What kind of question is that? We will always love each other," I replied. "We just got married so young that other things came into play. It happens."

Kaheem was no fool, and he was most certainly a replica of his dad. The boy spoke his mind with no hesitation. "You two aren't together, because of her. I heard the arguments, and I promise never to like her, Ma. I'll keep her away from my brothers and sister, I swear. I wouldn't even speak to her if I could get away with it, but you know Dad won't allow no disrespect."

Well, unfortunately for me, Kaheem's tidbit of knowledge on the matter opened the floodgates, and I spilled the beans like a lovesick fool. I gave my son way too much ammunition, and after he left the comfort of my home and entered his father's, he blasted him with all he had to give. Rahmel was pissed. He had a right to be. We had promised not to involve the kids, and dammit, I had upheld that with all my might, but I got weak. I just got caught up in the moment.

I can still remember being chastised by Rahmel like I was a fucking kid myself, and he put salt on an open wound by forbidding me to spend time with the boys anymore. He figured they had enough turmoil from being abandoned by their natural mother and then dealing with our divorce. He didn't need me to "make matters worse."

I was sick in the stomach. Loosing my grasp on those boys gave me the same sickening feeling I had gotten when I walked out my mother's door, leaving my siblings to fend for themselves. In a matter of months, my simple life had been turned completely upside down.

So what does all of this have to do with fucking? you may ask. Simply put, fucking saved me. It saved me from myself. It was as if I had discovered myself buried under years of mental suffocation, and I had now been transformed into a sexual diva that could woo any man she wanted. Hell, bitches, too, for that matter.

I spread my legs wide, took short, deep breaths, and then gave birth to the bad Sex Diva, Nina Tracy. Like the slave monkeys in the movie *The Wiz*, I unzipped who I was on the outside and finally let her step out to breathe. She inhaled the fresh air around her. I exhaled. Nina, like she would do to so many others, had taken my breath away.

Unlike the old me, Nina could walk into a room and have her pick of the litter. The confidence of my newfound sexuality flowed through my pores like a sweet perfume, and I felt like the Pied Piper leading my followers to my parlor. Seduction was a game, and for the first time in my life, I was winning. The power I felt was like a gateway drug. It was an awesome rush, but like any drug, there was the risk of addiction, not to mention the price I'd eventually have to pay for each hit.

Chapter Two

Be Patient

My sexual revolution was an experiment in the joy and pains that come from finding oneself through sexual exploration. For right now, let's just talk about the joy, the deep satisfaction and the heady excitement of living out one's deepest fantasies.

I'm sure there will be some who will wonder how a woman that calls herself a good momma could do some of the things I did, things that most women would have to admit that if there was a guarantee that no one would ever find out, they'd do in a heartbeat. And then there are others who will want to meet up with me to get some of that funk, that sweet, gushy stuff. So pour yourself a glass of wine and slip into a hot bubble bath. And for the record, it's okay to be touched by the experiences I'm about to share with you. Better yet, it's okay to touch yourself . . . yeah, right there.

* * *

"Three miles in forty-five minutes," I recited to myself. It wasn't my personal best, but it was pretty good, considering my meeting with the treadmill came at the tail end of an exhausting day.

The shower felt like heaven on earth. The steady stream of water beating my stiff joints was erasing all traces of sweat from my thick mane. Despite popular opinion, Mondays were the best.

One good thing about divorce was that no matter how ugly it was, when the kids were away with Daddy, I got the first real glimpse of "me time" that I had experienced in years.

This particular Monday was devoted to working my ass off to earn my keep on an ad campaign that promised to get me in line with a long-awaited promotion. Success in the workplace had become my passion. The more I worked, the less time I spent allowing my mind to replay all the events that had led up to my fucked-up divorce.

When the workday was done and the babies were off with Dad, I turned on my iPod and took my frustrations out on the treadmill. Ramping up the speed with a subtle incline, I challenged my body to a test of endurance. I ran to feel alive. I ran to feel free, and I ran to escape my troubled past and free myself of the pain.

Placing my palms against the warm tile, I leaned into the wall and planted my heels firmly on the floor, allowing the water to pour down over my stiff joints as I began a sequence of stretches to loosen up my sore limbs. Having received all the satisfaction I could from the hot shower in the workout facility's women's locker room, I turned the water off and reached for my towel and wrapped it securely around my chest. With the small towel the gym offered, I began to dry my hair. Slipping into my flip-flops, I made my way down the corridor of showers and into the locker area. It was quiet, with the exception of the late-night newscast being broadcast on the television monitors.

I made my way to the mirror to comb the tangled strands of my thick mane. Looking in the mirror, I wondered how my newly single life would play out for me and my children. It had only been four months since the divorce, but it felt like a lifetime.

I had gotten married so young that when I found myself divorced at the age of twenty-seven, I considered myself to be an old maid, an old maid that not even an old man would have any interest in. I'm smiling right now as I think back on just how wrong I was.

As I combed my hair, I allowed myself to admire the reflection in the mirror. "I guess I ain't so bad," I said out loud, shrugging my shoulders. My thick locks of hair fell well below my shoulders. My husband used to love running his hands through my ebony mane. Used to.

I leaned in closer to take a better look at myself. I ran my hands down my neck, and then I opened my towel slightly and admired my flat stomach. My caramel complexion remained unmarked after the birth of two children. A little advice from the elders and a few bottles of olive oil had gone a long way in keeping my skin taunt, healthy, and glowing.

I looked both ways to ensure that the coast was clear before I opened my towel completely for a full examination of the goods. Exercising had worked miracles, removing the extra fifteen pounds I had carried throughout my marriage; the stress diet—not eating for days and days—that comes with finding out your spouse is a lying cheat had helped.

I admired the firm breasts that had allowed my two small babies to suckle. They had withstood the trials of motherhood and appeared to be looking back at my inquiring eyes, as if to say, "Bitch, move on. There are no problems here."

My flat abs were far from a six-pack, but the sinewy line down my midsection and the appearance of two small muscles just below my ribs made me smile. My eyes then explored my full hips and round ass. Now these two areas, despite my attempts to reduce, were just as full and plump as Aphrodite herself. I recalled my attempts to exercise and reduce the girth of my hips and ass after the birth of my second child, Ariel. I smiled as I recalled my husband's comments.

"Uumm, girl, uh-uh. Keep that just the way it is," he had said flirtatiously. I had thought he meant it, so I kept it. Now I couldn't get rid of it for the life of me.

The span from my waist to my ass proved to be most disturbing in the dressing room. After my divorce, I began to experiment with the latest fashion trends, but to my dismay, I learned quickly that very few designers offered jeans that didn't need to be tailored for sistahs with dimensions like mine. I hate to admit it, and on top of that, it's very unlike me to be downright vain, but I loved the look of my ass in a fitted pair of jeans or capris.

Yes, I liked the attention. Hell, I yearned for it. For so long, I had gone without it, and now I was desperate to find out just what I had been missing. There is absolutely nothing wrong with a woman enjoying a little attention every now and again. And if all it took was a snug-fitting scoop-neck T-shirt and a pair of painted-on jeans to get it, so be it.

I had lived the past eight years sporting the dowdy clothing my husband thought was fit for a wife and mother. Little had I known, it was my husband's own little secret kryptonite. It kept any attention from any other man off me. And if I'm not mistaken, it kept my husband's attention off me as well. But as soon as he was out of the house, so was that pitiful wardrobe of mine. But it was soon replaced with one full of color and life, you know, something to draw a little attention to myself. And this new attention, oh yeah, I could definitely get used to it. I had taken careful pains, to transform myself into the type of woman I wanted to be all my life. From molding a new body to meticulously piecing together a new wardrobe I was taking baby steps towards meeting my goal. The Miracle Bra, got three of em, platforms that can go from the boardroom to the bedroom-love 'em, and did I mention the torture I put the little blond bitch through at the MAC counter until I could apply my makeup exactly the same way she did, maybe better? Two hours after my session I walked out of Nordstoms a couple of yards short of what I walked in with but seeing my reflection in the mirror and armed with the knowledge that I had made that little hussy earn her commission made my $200.00 money well spent. I solicted my BFF (best friend for life) Monica to be my personal shopper and together we transformed my look from mousy housewife to a high steppin' head turner. I loved the compliments I received and when I ran into folks I haven't seen in awhile the shock on there faces was priceless.

My ultimate satisfaction came when I strolled into Rahmel's kitchen to pick up the kids, he looked at me like I was a plate of smothered chicken, with a side of greens, macaroni and cheese, and cornbread. "Hey Mel, what up" I watch his Adam's apple travel the length of his neck as he tried to find his tongue. "Damn Nina, what'd you do?" As I proceeded to the door I gave him a winning smile, tossed back my hair and replied "oh nothing." I could hear his feet beat a path across the kitchen floor and as he shuffled to get a glimpse of my rearview. "Eat your heart out playa," I said with a satisfied grin.

I gave myself a wink and then hurriedly secured my towel back around my chest as sounds of life sprang from the shower area. I took another moment to lean into the mirror and give my face the same examination I had offered my body.

My high forehead was home to expertly arched eyebrows, which my best friend had insisted I keep up. Once I got them arched and admired how their new shape adorned my wide brown eyes, I was sure to schedule an appointment every two weeks for regular maintenance. This was a luxury that had never crossed my mind when I was busy tending to a husband and raising a family.

My caramel face was also home to a lusty pair of lips. I always loved the shape of them. I recalled being asked by many women how I lined my lips to give them their full, lusty appearance. Some of these women hinted at the idea of lip injections. I was glad to admit that this pair of smackers was all mine. Nice and full, with a perfect indentation on my upper lip.

I loved the way my MAC lip gloss made men want to beg me for a kiss.

High cheekbones and a delicate chin framed my face. Between my cheekbones was a perfectly sized nose. My neckline and shoulders begged for hot kisses down the length of my five-foot-four-inch frame. I hadn't fared so badly at all, and weekly visits to the gym had only served to create a truly defined visual feast.

I proceeded to my locker and slipped into a black one-piece swimsuit. I grabbed a dry towel from the rack and proceeded to indulge myself in the ultimate treat that I awarded my body after a thorough workout.

As I opened the door to the pool area, all was quiet. The Olympic-sized swimming pool was completely still. As my flip-flop-covered feet padded their way to the whirlpool tub, I sent up a quick prayer that I would be able to enjoy this treat all by my lonesome, that no intruders would come to invade the peace and serenity of just me, myself, and I.

I quickly discovered I was to have no such luck; my cohabitant was an old white man who couldn't possibly be in the gym to work out. It looked like he had trouble enough just staying alive. He gave me a toothless grin and nodded his head as if he was welcoming me into the heated waters. I slid off my flip-flops and began my climb down three warm tiled steps, pausing only long enough to remove my towel and lay it on the side of the whirlpool. As I straightened up and began my descent into the hot bubbles, I couldn't help but notice that grandpa was taking it all in, every last inch of me. I laughed to myself and inwardly thought, *Get it while you live, Papi. Now-shit!*

Gramps and I were apparently on the same mission. Clearly, he was taking in every nook and cranny of my body, and if I was a betting woman, I would put money on it that Gramps only came to the gym to get his kicks. *Well, Papa, when it comes to the hot tub, you and I are on the same page, because I, too, am here to get mine.*

I looked to the far end of the large whirlpool to see that the Old G and I were not alone. A healthy sister sat along the far wall, glaring at Grandpa like she wanted to get up and smack the taste out of his mouth. We met eyes and smiled at one another. She gave me a look that said, "Do you see this old white fool over here about to get a woody?" Knowing that sistah girl had my back offered me a certain sense of security. I made my way to my playground to enjoy the hot springs of the whirlpool.

I eased my way slowly into the depths of the hot bubbles. I softly purred, at only a pitch my ears could hear, as the steaming hot depths climbed up my thighs. Now this was truly heaven.

I made my way to my usual spot, glad to see it was ready and waiting for me. I sat on the hot, watery stoop, right across from Grandpa, and as I eased into position and began to close my eyes, I couldn't help but notice that I still had his undivided attention. I ignored him and just closed my eyes.

"Ummm Pedro, my lover," I said to myself. Now the term *Pedro* was coined on a trip to Jamaica with a few of my best girlfriends. While spending time at the poolside, one of my girls, Monica, fell in love with a waterspout that sent waves of water rushing into the pool. Well, in this case, the water just happened to hit Monica in just the right spot, if you get my drift. Every day, as soon as we were able to get a good couple of margaritas down, Monica was in position, holding on to the edge of the pool and pretending that she wasn't concentrating on the rapid waves of water vibrating her greedy clit. Thus, the term *Pedro* was coined. Pedro didn't need any time to get up or special instructions to stay in the right spot. All you had to do was position yourself in front of him, and he did all the work.

Well, it just so happened that I rediscovered Pedro back home in the gym's whirlpool. I positioned myself right above a spout, which sprang to life between my thighs and offered my clit a healthy dose of pressure. As I situated myself in the hot bubbles, I let my mind wander to the training session I had had just two nights before with Dante.

Dante was a friend of a friend who had volunteered his personal training services during my "time of need." Although we had traveled in the same circle for years, this was my first one-on-one encounter with Dante, and having him this close proved to be quite disconcerting to my senses.

I had always thought that Dante was sexy as hell, with a great personality, and somehow, in that dirty little mind of mine, I'd imagined him to be somewhat of a freak. But my relationship with him was strictly professional. At least that's how it was supposed to be, anyway.

My training session with him had proved to be sheer torture. The more demands he put on me, the more my traitorous cunt purred for satisfaction. I couldn't help but imagine his thick lips on my pussy, my hands in his short, dark 'fro, and his fat dick standing at attention. If our relationship was supposed to be so professional, then you might wonder how I knew he was packing. Then go ahead and ask away. I've got plenty of answers.

During my second set of squats, Dante had stood his sexy ass in front of me like a drill sergeant. There I was, standing, with my legs hip-width apart, shoulders back and chin up. As I dipped into squat position, I came face-to-pipe with Dante's package.

Oh my God! Each squat was both pleasure and pain. My inner devil wanted to throw caution to the wind, drop the damn weights, pull down Dante's loose-fitting sweats, and fill my mouth with his dick. Needless to say, I didn't, which was why I was sitting in that whirlpool, getting off on just the thought of him.

Damn, damn, damn. Nina, get it together! I instructed myself. My juices were flowing, and my bottom lip hung open as if I was summoning his loins to my lips like a Scooby snack. As the bubbles danced at my thighs and worked their magic on my clit, I relaxed into a fantasy and allowed my mind to wander.

From the shadows of my mind, he was there. Five feet eleven inches and brown skinned, with a tight, compact frame. His sinewy body was pure muscle, and his handsome face was what dreams were made of.

In my mind, he came to me as I lay naked, soaking up the sun. A vision in white linen, he quickly tore off his shirt and bent to kiss me passionately, licking my lips, thirsty for more of my sweet offerings. His fiery kisses didn't stop at my mouth, though. He blazed a path down my neck and to the small, round peaks of my dark, hard nipples. He paused just long enough to admire them before his tongue traced the outline of one hungry nipple right before it disappeared into his mouth.

He was an expert lover. He sucked it just right, and when I couldn't take it anymore, he moved on to the next. My body arched to meet his lips, and when the teasing became too fierce, he moved farther south to find the center of my being. His mouth teased my thighs as his strong hands clasped a handful of ass. My legs parted to meet him, but he didn't give me what I wanted right away.

"Be patient, Nina," Dante said seductively.

Slowly, and with great ease, he licked the outer lips of my soul and circled his tongue patiently until he was rewarded with the feel of an inpatient little clit, waiting to be sucked. The impatient little bitch got exactly what she wanted, too. He never did her wrong.

I looked down at his black Afro, glistening in the sunlight, and his handsome face, working magic on my pussy. The combinations of licks and sucks were all I could stand, and I was sent overboard when he slid one long finger into the tight, hot cavern of my being, teasing my insides while he controlled me with his lips.

I reached down with one hand and clung to the nape of his neck. I pulled him in as close as I could. I pulled him in with the intent of making sure he didn't miss a spot. Not one single inch. Just when the world started to spin around me and the fire building within me was about to blaze into an inferno, he released me and sent me crashing back to reality.

"What the hell!" I yelled out. "Damn it, you bastard."

He laughed at my frustration and stood up, casually loosening the drawstring of his pants. They slid down his chiseled thighs and landed at his feet. The sight of him was enough to stop my tantrum long enough to admire the view.

"Greedy bitch, are you hungry for more?" He crouched to greet me with passionate kisses. "Do you like the taste of your own pussy?" he asked.

"Uh-huh," I moaned as I desperately reached for his swollen dick.

My fingers wrapped around him—barely—and the girth made me tingle with anticipation.

"Feed me some dick, Papi . . . pleassse," I begged.

"Anything for you, baby," Dante responded, with a grin.

The huge head of his dick parted my pussy lips with expert precision. I felt my body give to allow him all the room he needed. And my tight pussy clung to him like my life depended on it.

Dante slung his hips and controlled my movement, sending me spinning back into his flaming inferno. He grabbed my hips and rolled me on top of him, all the while kissing me and offering me his tongue.

While one strong hand grabbed a firm piece of luscious booty, the other slid into my ass and caused my hips to move harder. I needed to feel all of him. Damn, it was good, and I rotated my hips in a desperate attempt to get all of it inside me and to spread my wetness over every inch of his rock-hard dick. I could feel the pleasure mounting, so I arched my back toward the sunny heavens and let out a ragged, muted cry. "Aayyhhh!"

Despite the hot wetness of the whirlpool spa, reality hit me like a smack in the face. Realizing my moan was not imagined, my pleasure quickly turned into sheer shame and humiliation. How much of the fantasy that had taken place in my head had I verbalized?

My eye's flew open to meet the wide eyes of Grandpa, who looked like he would fall face forward into the pool if he leaned any closer. He apparently had gotten more than he had bargained for when he set out for a peaceful float in the hot tub. My little performance had him on the verge of busting a nut.

I glanced in the direction of sister girl, who was waving her arms slowly in the swirl of hot bubbles. She had furrowed eyebrows and was giving me a look that was telling me that my black ass oughta be ashamed of myself.

"This is bullshit," I muttered under my breath as I laid my head back onto the ledge of the whirlpool. I shut my eyes, with the hope that when they reopened, my companions would disappear.

I could almost feel tears of frustration burning in my eyes. How the hell was it that all this sexuality I felt on the inside had never made its way into my bedroom? Yeah, my husband and I had had sex on the regular. We had even christened a few rooms in the house, such as the shower, the kitchen, you know, the usual places. Despite a very active sex life, though, I had always found myself masturbating as the fantasies played over and over again in my mind.

I just knew that there had to be something better than a make-believe world of exotic lovemaking. I mean, where the fuck was this Erotic City our purple majesty had sung about, convincing us that it was a real place, like Fantasy Island or some shit? Or had even Prince tricked us into thinking the place was real, when all the while it had merely been in his head, too?

For me, Pedro was no longer going to do the trick. If I was going to get fucked in public, I was going to at least be in the presence of a real, live dick.

I eased my way out of the whirlpool and grabbed my towel, without a second glance in the direction of my pool mates. As I dried off, I made a promise to myself. *Nina, even if you don't get a damn thing out of this single life you've suddenly found yourself living, you are going to get your kicks before you even think about getting into another damn relationship.*

I made that vow without a thought as to how I was going to go about finding my "kicks." The only thing I knew for sure was that freaky shit was happening somewhere, and it wasn't about to go down too much longer without my black ass up in the mix.

I made my way back to the locker room and pulled my things out of my locker. I threw on a black Nike sweat suit and covered my damp head with a black skullcap. I made quick work of tossing my work clothes into the gym bag and bundling up before I headed out into the cool winter air.

All my damn life I had been dedicated to taking care of family. It might have been the only way out of a bad situation, but I had made the best of it, and I thought I had found what I wanted.

All I wanted was a man who was as open to exploration as I was. One who wanted to worship my body like a temple and experiment with me and enjoy some of my most deep-seated fantasies, such as being with a woman.

I wanted to feel the softness of another female's breasts against mine, and I wanted a full supporting cast of onlookers to watch as I was pleasured to no end. Please believe that I didn't know where to go or what I would find in my quest for satisfaction. The only thing that made sense to me was that despite the heartbreak of my divorce, this was my chance to be a freak . . . a bona fide bad girl with no one to answer to but my damn self!

Well, that cold night, as I made my way to my SUV in the frigid January, I looked to the stars and tried to imagine what was in store for me. It was only a matter of time before my fantasies began to manifest themselves. I knew it. I could just feel it, because the heavens don't lie.

Chapter Three

BFFs

I hurried through a maze of parked cars, trying desperately to dodge the freezing winds and the wrath of my best friend, Monica. I was fifteen minutes late for our lunch date, and her prompt ass was sure to give me an earful about it.

As soon as I stepped into the entryway of the Citizen's Bar, I met the cool gaze of Monica, posted up at a bar-side table, with her back straight, looking like she was fit to be tied. I had to laugh at the picture she created, because she was clearly putting on her best pout.

I gestured to the hostess and gave Monica a wave as I made my way to her table. "Go on and get it over with, Monica," I told her. "I'm all ears."

For once in our seventeen years of friendship, she let me off the hook without comment. Her stiff demeanor suddenly loosened up as she waved her hand and said, "Girl, please. You straight. I ordered a Long

Island and checked off my 'Shit To Do' list while I waited for you," she said, taking a sip of her Long Island. "I know you've got a lot on your plate these days."

I was shocked and relieved to hear those words. The last thing I needed was the added stress of a perturbed best friend. My life had been spinning past me, and I was beginning to think that no one had noticed.

"Let's talk about that," I said, pausing only long enough to order my own top-shelf Long Island. "Lately, Brent's ass has been pouring on the pressure at work, which is a good thing, just at a really crazy time," I complained to her. Brent was my direct supervisor. "In the meantime, my poor babies have had their whole life turned upside down and are getting adjusted to their father and me living apart, and I'm just trying to maintain some balance in their lives." I sipped on my Long Island. Actually, it was more like a gulp. Hell, I needed to be buzzed.

"You know, these babies always had their momma and daddy under one roof," I continued, "and they are just not adjusting well to shuttling back and forth between two households."

Monica took a second to absorb the information and proceeded to ask, "So have you managed to multitask some dick in your bed when they little asses is at they daddy's house?"

A stream of girlish giggles followed, and as usual, my girl seemed to have read my mind. The waitress came over and took our food orders. Then I proceeded to answer Monica's question.

"Girl, ain't no pipe been in my bed yet. But I do have a pipe prospect," I told her.

"Well, now shit," Monica chimed in. "A prospect is better than nothing. But what's wrong with him, though? I mean, something must be wrong if he's only a prospect. You been a virgin for the second time long enough not to have let him hit that."

See, that's why Monica was my BFF. She held the same point of view as I did when it came to a woman's entitlement to some dick without any backlash, the same way men got pussy.

Monica's round face was framed by shoulder-length hair streaked with blond highlights, which she had paid a grip for. The chunky highlights served only to accent Monica's hazel eyes and flawless complexion. This child didn't have a mark on her golden skin. Monica's momma was the first to warn us that if we kept falling and "playing like boys," we were going to have ugly, scarred-up legs. Well, Monica must have followed her momma's words by the book, because she could have been in a Noxzema ad.

I could recall being young and hearing the boys in the neighborhood comment that if it wasn't for Monica's eyes, she would be "real average." Monica didn't have a huge, black girl booty or tits that stood out in a crowd, but she made up for what some might have thought was lacking with a winning personality.

My girl did not meet any strangers, and everywhere we went, she knew somebody who wanted to get close to her. She was the girl in school that participated in every school activity there was and had friends in all of the cliques. My girl was the coolest ever. She was a sports fanatic, so the boys loved her, and she was a fashion diva, diving into the pages of *Vogue.* She was buying shit for the winter that was on the runways of Fashion Week in the spring.

"So go ahead. Tell me," said Monica. "What's wrong with him? He in a wheelchair? Is the brotha's back broke? Why ain't he hit the skins?"

Another stream of giggles, and it appeared our tiny table was starting to get too much attention.

"Ain't nothing wrong with him," I assured her. "He just ain't made any serious moves, and I am not one to force the issue. You know me."

In actuality, Monica would have had my head if she knew the tidbit of information I had kept under lock and key for the past two days. My mystery man Monte had stopped by to chill and watch a movie with me the other night, after the kids had gone to bed. He had a couple of bootleg CDs and a bottle of wine in hand. We settled down in the family room to watch the movie, and, well, one thing led to another. There was no score, but second base was better than nothing. With my head resting on Monte's rock-hard bicep and the smooth buzz I got after my second glass of Riesling, I was prepared to be a little bit risqué.

Along with charm, Monte had a luscious pair of smackers. Looking him in the eyes, I licked my lips in a come hither fashion. He got the hint. Right before he reached my lips, he pulled back, studying me like he was feeling me out.

"I won't bite," I said, and that was all the ammunition he needed.

We attacked each other like long-lost lovers. It had been so long for me. I don't know what his excuse was. Monte lifted me onto his lap and pulled up my shirt, shoving my bra around my neck. I inhaled sharply as he wrapped those sexy-ass lips around my nipple and licked a happy trail from one breast to the other.

With his strong arms securely cupping my ass, I leaned back to allow him a wider playing field and closed my eyes as I relished the heated kisses he was blazing down my stomach and onto my sides. I just kept telling myself that it had been so long and that I needed to just let myself go. It was my time. I refused to allow myself to think about the consequences. I refused to think about how I would feel about it in the morning. I deserved to be cherished, and so far, Monte was the HNIC (Head Nigga In Charge) of the cherishing.

Monte's mouth was on fire. He blazed a path back to my lips, and without notice, he rose to his feet, securely wrapping his arms around me and laying me on the sofa. I made quick work of getting rid of my T-shirt and bra, and I was on my way to the drawstring of my loose cotton gauchos when Monte's disrobing distracted me from my mission.

I stopped what I was doing to appreciate the man before me. He unbuttoned his shirt like a Chippendale looking for a tip. He was intentionally trying to tease me, but that was okay. I slid my right hand down my pants and massaged my needy snatch as I watched him undress through my lashes. His button-up discarded, he tossed his wife beater by the wayside in one swoop. As he stood before me, I was transfixed by the size of his body. I admired his reddish brown skin, which gave the appearance of a year-round tan, and I wondered what my hands would feel like grasping those massive shoulders, which accentuated a chest that was so wide, I could crawl up on it and sleep. Monte was a big boy.

Standing in Timberlands and jeans, Monte stepped out of his boots one foot at a time and unhooked his belt, letting his loose-fitting jeans drop to the floor with a thud. He had the body of a nigga that had dangled a few brothers from a balcony a time or two, so I couldn't wait to see what tricks he had in store for little old me. There Monte stood, with his socks and boxers. I didn't have long to wait. My fingers pressed against my clit, slowly circling her and prepping Mommy for some real stimulation. Monte grabbed the elastic of his boxers and confidently lowered them to show me my prize. He stood up, basking in the light of the television to reveal a wiggling, hard dick that, despite my wildest dreams of what he had to offer, managed to be real fucking average.

Sucks to be me, right? It would have been too much like right for King Kong to jump out of his pants, huh? We had come this far. The way I saw it, my ass was so tight, I could barely squeeze all six inches of my vibrator inside of me. This average chumpy would have to do. All I could hope for was that he knew how to work it. Monte walked the short distance to the sofa.

"Shut the door," I told him, "and lock it." The last thing I needed was to have my first piece in what seemed like forever interrupted by a curious little person who heard Mommy making noises.

As Monte was on his way over to me after closing and locking the door, I was still working on my clit to make sure that one way or another, I busted a nut.

"Monte, baby, you did bring protection with you, right?"

He stopped dead in his tracks and looked dumbfounded. Shit, fuck, damn! His face said it all. "Nah, baby, but I'll pull out. No worries, Ma. I got you."

No the hell you don't, was the response dancing through my mind.

"Well, in that case . . ." The devil on my left shoulder talked a good game. We had come too far to back away now. The angel attacked him with a vengeance. The faces of my children flashed before me. Fuck the dumb, my fingers had made me a self-service station thus far. I stuck with the chick sprouting wings. "In that case, baby, I'll have to take a rain check. As much as I want you right now, it's not worth the risk. I don't get down without a condom, so next time come prepared."

Monte looked defeated. He made a few feeble attempts to reason with me. I let him carry on his own conversation with himself about wanting me so bad he could . . . yada, yada, yada. Save it for another broad. The floodgates were no longer open.

Monte managed to accept defeat, and I tossed the pillows aside to allow him some room on the couch. After he got into position, I curled up beside him, and we just lay there, staring at the walls, reflecting on what had just gone down. After a short while, Monte found his tongue. "You know, Nina, I really dig you, baby. I'm digging the way we flow. And to keep it real, I'm glad it didn't go down like that just now, you know?"

Hmmm. This was a switch coming from a dude. I wanted him to tell me more . . . and he did. "You know, baby. I handle my business, and above all else, I take care of mine. I need you to know that. I would never disrespect you. You're different; you got a lot of class about yourself, and you represent a brother well. Believe that. I can see us going somewhere, you know?"

Oh my God. Maybe I didn't want to hear more. Was this beginning to sound like a Ja Rule song or what? I was not only not on Monte's wavelength, I was getting turned off real fast. So rather than say some shit I would regret because I was frustrated by the lack of pipe, and in order to keep this thing going, I just kind of punked out.

"Let's just take our time and see what happens, how about that?" I wasn't in the mood to get into a relationship discussion, especially when I knew I wasn't in it to win it, you know.

Monica would be laid out if she knew I had come within an inch of some pipe and didn't get laid. In her own words, condoms are the enemy, so she would have gone for the gusto with no hesitation.

"Okay, bitch, it's about time to start sending out some fermions," said Monica. She sighed as she sipped on her drink. "Look, I saw Rahmel with that bitch he left you for at the movies."

Yes, Monica said it right. That rat bastard had left me for another woman. Some nerve. After he had custom made me, he went out and got another model. This motherfucker had gone from black Barbie to motherland Barbie, and had left my ass on misfit island with the rest of the castaways.

Monica rolled her eyes and sucked her teeth. "When I saw their asses together, I thought to myself, 'Leaving my girl was the worst decision you ever made.'" Monica looked me dead in the eye. "Now I want you to move on so his suffering can begin. Let him see you all hugged up with another dude."

Lord knows Monica meant well, I know she did,

but her words cut deep. Every time I thought I had moved ten steps forward, someone had to bring up that rat bastard and his little home-wrecking ho and mess up my flow.

Monica must have sensed my mood swing. "I'm sorry, Nina. I know you asked to be kept out of the loop on the Rahmel sightings, but I just want to give you ammunition to move on. Anyway, back to this potential brother you are considering as a prospect. Tell me about him."

A shift in subjects was definitely past due, so I gladly obliged and replied to her inquiry. "His name is Monte, but everybody calls him Mo. He's an East-sider, so his steelo is definitely new to us."

Monica interrupted. "Speak for yourself, Nina. I have been single in this city for three years, chick. Trust me, the only person in our clique that East Side boys are new to is you."

I rolled my eyes and proceeded with my description. "Anyway, he definitely has class. We've gone to some really nice places. I love a brother who knows about fine dining."

Monica interrupted again. "Did he leave a tip that was more than five percent?"

I chuckled despite myself. But the matter of leaving tips was a pet peeve for me and my clique of girlfriends. There were just too many brothers who thought that tipping was a courtesy and not a requirement of a good dining experience. You know what I'm talking about: the ones that cause a girl to reach in her purse and make up the difference. It's not a big deal, just a sign of class in my book.

"He left a twenty percent tip," I told Monica. "Girl, I had made a mental note to myself about that one.

But overall, I really enjoy my time with Mo. We laugh, talk shit, all that good stuff."

Monica eyed me suspiciously. "So . . ." Her words trailed off. She picked them back up again immediately, though. "What's the problem, chick?"

I squirmed in my seat like I was being interrogated by the police. I hadn't even consciously admitted the problem to myself, but the moment of truth was here. My girl was not going to allow me to get up and walk out of here without an explanation.

"Well, first and foremost, he owns his own business, which is great. I'm all about the black man doing his thang."

Monica looked at me, with one eyebrow in the air, waiting impatiently for the other shoe to drop, so I unlaced it and prepared to throw it.

"On the flip side of that, though, he has got too much time on his hands," I confessed, "and I have been around hustlers long enough to know one when I see one."

Monica leaned back in her chair and threw her arms up like she couldn't believe I had fixed my mouth to say those words. "Nina Gabrielle Tracy. I know you're not discriminating against a brother making his money, considering your uncles were the *biggest* bunch of hustlers in the city when we were still playing double Dutch."

Monica was right. My male fam was and still could be a bunch of hoodlums if need be, but she was missing my point. "Hey, I'm not hating on how he gets his change, by no means, but I have Ariel and Miles to consider now. I can't have no drama unfold at my front door because of my associations. I ain't got nothing but the rest of my life for them babies. Now shit!"

Monica rolled her eyes and looked me in my face like I had lost my damn mind. "Nina, ain't nobody said you got to marry Monte's ass. Just because the only real dick you had belonged to a no-good snake in the grass that you married don't mean you got to marry the next piece you get. Just let Monte slide in late and leave early. You used to love the little dope boys when we were young, buying you Fendi bags and picking your fast ass up from school. If Rahmel's righteous ass hadn't snatched you up and put a head wrap on your head, you would have been well on your way to being a dope man's bitch." Monica added in a serious tone, "Uh-huh. I was there, remember?" Monica was a regular operator of information and didn't forget shit.

"You're right, Monica," I told her. "I took full advantage of my dope boy privileges back then, but that was well before I became a mother of two. It's different when you have other little lives at stake than when you're putting just your own on the line."

I was glad to see some relief on the way when my grilled seafood salad made its way to the table. As I focused all of my attention on my food, Monica casually picked up a chicken wing from her appetizer platter and continued her speech.

"Nina, I am not even gon' front. It's some sorry pickins we got to choose from out here, but you just got out of a what, seven plus, eight-year marriage, which happened before you knew what you were getting yourself into. Trust me, baby, when I say that the last thing I want is for you to meet Mr. Right at this point in the game. You need to be free and to find yourself first. Get to know who you are." Her voice became stern out of concern for my well-being. "Nina, stop being so serious, and let your hair down. Stop dressing like you got something to hide, and live a little, baby!"

Monica was right. Life had been all about responsibility for me, but that was because I kept finding myself in positions where I always had to be the responsible one.

I was proud of my accomplishments. Proud that I had become a home owner before I had even turned twenty-four. Proud of the strides I had made to distance myself from my impoverished childhood of welfare and food stamps. I had made it as far as I was concerned. I had done everything I had set out to do, but yet something was still missing.

I took extra time to chew my salad while I marinated on what Monica had said. And everything she had to say made sense.

"You're right," I finally agreed. "I'm not trying to marry the man. And I do really, really need some pipe right about now." There were those girlish giggles again.

"Uh-huh," Monica added.

"But you made a valid point. It has been one man since I can remember, so excuse me if I don't fuck the first half-decent man I meet." Before Monica could respond, I added, "Did I mention that he lived with his momma?"

Monica almost choked on her chicken wing. "Oh, hell no! What the hell kind of two-dollar, fine-dining hustler you dealing with?"

We both commenced cracking up.

"See what I'm talking about?" I said, shaking my

head. "I think I need a rule book for this dating thang. This is way too complicated," I said in between laughs.

"Enough about him. Let's talk about your birthday. So what's the plans? Are we going to have a crazy, ridiculous party? Is the clique just going to meet out somewhere and party like rock stars or what? Let me know, Mama, 'cause you know I'm down for whatever and I got you." As if Monica could see the celebration going down right before her very eyes, she added all in one breath, "Ohhh, and you better make sure you have something fly to wear. All eyes need to be on you birthday girl."

"Nikki made arrangements for us to have a little somethin', somethin' at the Piccadilly. You know the owner is her brother's boy. And, yes I am going to have something fly to wear, and I'll have you know, I've upgraded my wardrobe significantly. I got my head out of the sand. Just keep watching my back."

"That goes without saying," Monica said, with a wink.

We finished our lunch date, catching up on family drama and the good time we planned to have on my b-day. As we wrapped ourselves up to prepare for the elements, Monica turned to me and said, "Nina, you've always lived for everybody else, even them babies, and I know Ariel and Miles are your pride and joy, but you got to take a little time for you . . . and your pussy."

We laughed our way, arm in arm, to our cars. Monica was bound and determined for me to meet up with Big Pipe Mike, even if she had to tie me down and pay somebody. Hmmm, that tying down thing doesn't sound half bad.

Anyway, it was then, at that lunch date with Monica, that I knew I had to step out of my shell to get what I wanted out of life. I didn't want to make any major waves. I just wanted to make a little noise and then run for cover. I had always envied Monica's single status. With no commitments or kids, she was doing the damn thing. Monica had no qualms about loving a man and leaving him, and she had some downright dirty stories about what had gone down on some of her trips. I decided to throw caution to the wind and step into this new year of my life like a grown-ass woman on a mission. I was past due for making some major changes in my life if I was going to get everything out of it that I had ever imagined.

By the time I celebrated my next birthday, I wanted to be celebrating more than just another year added to my existence. I wanted to celebrate the completion of self. I had denied myself long enough. It was something that deep down inside of me, I had always longed to do. And now I had planned on accomplishing it. So with a hope and a prayer, I decided it was time to begin my quest.

Chapter Four

Me, Myself and I

Here it was, the morning of my twenty-eighth birthday, the day my girls and I were going to party the night away in celebration of my first birthday in years as a single woman. As I woke up and stretched, I couldn't help but think back to the dream I had enjoyed the night before. A wet dream no less. I felt good. I felt new and refreshed.

A smile spread across my face as the sun began to rise and peek in through my blinds, kissing my soft caramel skin. The early morning sun rays beckoned me over to the window. I pulled the satin sheets off of me and made my way over to the window, cracking open the blinds just slightly, just slightly enough so that the sun and I could connect and share a moment alone together. It was as if I was the sun's favorite and it wasn't shining on anybody else that morning but me.

I closed my eyes and took in the heat that it was

providing on this cold winter morning. I exhaled as I began to caress my body. Before I knew it, my hands had made their way down to my tender clit. I pressed my legs together, tightening my grip. I had almost forgotten what it was like to be touched, not in a moment of heated lust, but in a moment of solace.

I stood at the window, set on pleasing myself, not caring what passerby, if any, happened to look up my way and witness the act. This was my "me time."

I gently massaged my clit with one hand and rubbed my breasts with the other. I could feel my nipples harden through the chiffon nightie.

"Mmmm," I moaned, licking my lips, taking my time to truly enjoy myself.

After wiping the dripping juices from between my thighs, I went back over to the bed and collapsed backwards as if I was falling backwards into a swimming pool on a hot summer day.

"You've come a long way, baby," I said out loud. I allowed myself the luxury of just lying in bed for a few minutes while I reflected on the past year. It had been rough, but I had pulled through. For some reason, my birthday was symbolic of crossing the finish line after a triathlon. I can't explain why; I just felt like I had earned a new lease on a new and improved Nina.

My phone rang. I glanced at the clock and wondered who could be calling me before 8:00 a.m. It didn't take long to figure it out once I checked out my caller ID. My girl Tee was always up and about at some ghastly hour. She was a cookie cutter suburbanite, up jogging with her damn dog at the crack of dawn, so her early morning phone call was no surprise.

"What's up, chick?" I answered the phone just as

perky as I knew she would be on the other end of the line.

"Happy birthday to you, happy birthday to you . . ."

No, she didn't sing the entire song. I could hear her daughter playing backup singer, and their duet put an instant smile on my face.

Tee and I were like oil and water, but somehow we managed to click. Tee was raised in the hood like the rest of us, but she acted like she had grown up with a silver spoon in her mouth. If you didn't know her from way back in the day, you'd swear she had led a privileged life. But don't let the façade fool you; she could get downright hood rat in less than a minute flat. I guess that was a big part of where we failed to see eye to eye. Where Tee was okay with rubbing elbows with the rich and not so famous, I kept it real and didn't mind telling any of her uppity friends to step the fuck off. Nevertheless, that was my girl.

"Thank you, girl. You are the first birthday call I got."

Tee loved to be acknowledged but acted like it was no big deal. "Girl, no biggie. That's what girls are for. Now, is it still on tonight? I got me a cute outfit I been waiting to wear."

Why did all my chicks have to be divas? "I can already tell I'm gon' have to represent. You and Monica can't be trying to upstage the birthday girl, now shit!" We shared a laugh. "It's still on. We're meeting around eight at the Piccadilly. We will be out in full force. We representing tonight!" I could hardly contain my excitement. This was my first grown and sexy get-together in all my adult years.

"Well, all right. Let me get prepared for the ghetto girls." Tee held no punches when it came to her "tolerating" the rest of my crew. She and Monica jockeyed for position when it came to me, but both of them were my girls. I couldn't have one without the other. Tee spread knowledge, and she schooled me on working the room with the elite crowd. Both were well-educated black women, and whether Tee wanted to admit it or not, both were as ghetto as red Kool-Aid when it came down to it.

"Tee, can't you play nice in the sandbox for once? After a drink or two, you and Monica will be talking shit and trying to move in on each other's territory."

"Whatever. Hey, don't worry about me. I always maintain my composure. Anyway, I just wanted to give you a shout out before I start my day. I'll see you tonight."

"Thanks for the call. Love ya," I said.

"I know," was Tee's only reply. She was an uptight bitch, but that was my girl.

Today it wasn't so bad getting up and crawling out from under the cozy layers of my down comforter. I went and peeked into Ariel's room to find she had already vacated the premises. Upon further inspection, I made my way down to Miles's room to find both brother and sister fast asleep. I allowed myself to be absorbed by the sweet aura coming from their angelic little faces.

This new tradition of crawling into bed with her brother must have come from their time spent with Dad. My only guess was that Dad had company, and Ariel wasn't invited. I never bothered to ask; the simple fact that Miles and Ariel were sharing space with no arguments was fine by me.

"Hey, babies, time to wake up," I whispered, taking a seat at the edge of the bed. Their little eyes flickered, but they held on to the last moments of sleep for all it was worth. "Miles and Ari, come on. Time to wake up." I allowed them a few minutes of bonus sleep. As usual, Miles was the first to come to life.

"Hey, Mom," he whispered, with a frog in his little voice. "Happy birthday."

Upon hearing the words, Ariel opened her eyes, fully awake. "Happy birthday, Mommy!"

"Oh my goodness. What am I going to do with all this love this early in the morning?" I leaned forward to get a hug and kiss from both of them and then got to the business of getting them ready for the day.

Once I got them both in motion, I changed into some sweats and a sports bra and loaded up the eight-minute Tae Bo workout CD. I just needed a quick dose of adrenalin to get my blood pumping and prepare me for my workday.

After my workout, I checked on the kids, helped Ariel tie her shoes, brushed Miles's head, and jumped in the shower. Today was going to be a good day. As always, I spent my time in the shower scrubbing my body and thanking God for another day of life and for my healthy babies. As I reached for my towel and started to dry off, I heard a knock at the door.

"Mommy, we have a surprise for you," Ariel sang out.

"Shut up, Ari. You ain't supposed to tell her we got a surprise!" Miles scolded.

"I can tell her whatever I want, Miles!" Ariel hissed in a high-pitched whisper.

I secured my towel around my chest and opened the door, interrupting their exchange. "Well, what have we got here?" I asked.

Startled, it took them a nanosecond to regain their composure before they yelled, "Surprise!"

I was greeted by the biggest bowl of Fruity Pebbles I had ever seen in my life. Back in the day, we would have gotten our butts kicked for pouring all that cereal, knowing we wouldn't eat it all before it got soggy. Nevertheless, I was gracious. "Oh my goodness, thank you very much!" I accepted the bowl that Miles offered me and ate a heaping spoonful. "Thank you, babies. Fruity Pebbles are my favorite," I said between chews.

After breakfast, Miles and Ariel presented me with cards they each had created. Miles also gave me a poem written by Kaheem, which he had kept tucked in his book bag for the past three days, since he left his father's house. The poem read:

"Mom is"
by *Kaheem Tracy*
Mom is rice, macaroni, string beans. MMMM mom is some hot chicken wings. Mom is cool. Mom rules. Mom is a person that went to school. Mom is ashy when she gets out of the pool. Mom is all that. You know what else my mom is? My mom is BLACK!

I love you always, Mom
Love, Kaheem

That boy had the red, black, and green in his genes, that was for sure. I was happy to see that he had also, despite everything, kept a piece of me. That little boy was something special; he was going to be a force to be reckoned with some day. I hugged Ariel and Miles with all my might. "You tell Kaheem that was a very, very special poem, and I will always treasure it. You tell Kaheem and Omari that I love them this much." I spread my arms out wide. "And make sure you give them a big bear hug, like Mommy is givin' you right now. Promise?"

"We promise," came from Ariel.

"I promise, Mom," said my little, big man, Miles.

"Now let's get bundled up and out the door. Go get your coats," I said.

We headed out the door and made our first stop, the Wee Winkle Learning Center, Ariel's preschool.

"Give Mommy a kiss and promise to be a big girl, okay? I'll see you on Tuesday." This little, crazy chick wasn't having it.

"On Tuesday? But, Mommy, we're supposed to be with you this weekend, not Daddy. And what about your birthday? We're supposed to eat cake together!" Ariel emphasized her case by stomping her foot firmly on the floor.

"Now, Ariel, stop pouting," I said.

"Why, Mommy? It's not ladylike?" Ariel was as sarcastic as a four-year-old going on sixteen could get.

"Right. It's not ladylike, and it will get you popped," I reminded her. She looked down at the floor, ashamed but she had reinforcements on the way.

Miles chimed in. "Mom, we want to be with you this weekend. It's Thursday. If we stay with Daddy, we won't see you for a long, long time." They were killing me softly, but I had to stay strong.

"Listen, hasn't your Momma always been there for you?" They shook their heads. "And doesn't Mommy have the right to have some time to herself on her birthday and rest? Being a Mommy is a big job, the biggest job in the whole, wide world, you feel me? Ain't no Daddy that can do what mommies do, no matter how hard they try. Now, I promise to call every day, and if you want some Mommy time, you can pick up the phone and call me. How about that?"

I'll admit it, laying the Mommy guilt trip on the kids was pretty low, but I had some catching up to do. Besides, Rahmel had been such an absentee father, with his community events and side fucking, this past year, he needed to spend some damn quality time. Miles's drop-off at his school went much smoother. I looked at him in the rearview mirror as I pulled in the parking lot.

"Where's your head at?" I asked.

Turning his attention toward me, he traced an imaginary line from his small forehead to mine. "My head is right here with you, Mommy," he recited like a champ.

"That's Momma's little, big man. Gimme some." We smacked five for good measure. "Now remember to take care of your sister and call me, okay?"

Miles slid out of the truck and landed solidly on two feet, gave me the thumbs-up, and yelled out, "I promise. Love you, Mom, and happy, happy birthday!"

I blew him a kiss good-bye. As always, Miles caught it with no problem. I watched him run down the sidewalk and disappear through the big red doors and into the school.

My workday flew by, with one pleasant surprise after another. I arrived in the office to find my small corner workstation had been taken over by a huge, colorful bouquet of balloons hovering over my small desk. My coworkers had become a second family, and I appreciated their acknowledgment. During the course of the day, I got a ton of love via e-mail and voice mail and a very special delivery from my mom. It was a beautiful array of wildflowers, with a very special note.

My little black Gerber baby is all grown up. You've blossomed into a remarkable woman. I can hardly believe you're mine. I love you more than you'll ever know.

Shine, baby, shine.

Love, Mom

We had our differences, but that was still my Mommy. The second-best call I got was from Monte. He did a modern-day rendition of the classic moment when Marilyn Monroe serenaded JFK with a very seductive happy birthday song.

My workday flew by. It could be because I hardly bothered to work. I took a two-hour lunch to get a manicure and put the finishing touches on my outfit. I had several phone calls and folks stopping by my desk, so before I knew it, it was time to go. I had barely even touched my computer today.

Pulling in front of my house, I was greeted with a pleasant surprise. A limousine was parked by the curb. No sooner had I pulled in the driveway and parked than the driver hopped out and greeted me.

"Ms. Tracy, my name is Antoine Hill, and I have the pleasure of being your driver this evening."

Okay, what was this all about? I did not expect this. I shook Antoine's hand and then commenced getting some details.

"Nice to meet you, Antoine. Now if you don't

mind my asking, who should I thank for this unexpected surprise?" I guess he figured I'd ask.

"I was hired by a Mr. Mo' Daddy. He also sent a big box to be opened by you only. If you'll step in the house, it will only take me a moment to retrieve it. I don't want to have a beautiful woman like yourself standing out in the cold."

I made my way to the front door and pulled out my cell phone at the same time to give Nikki a call. As soon as she picked up, I said, "Girrll, you ain't gonna believe this!" I gave her the details and let her know another surprise was on its way to the house.

No sooner had I spoken the words than there was Antoine, knocking at my screen door. Opening the door, I was handed a large box wrapped with gold leaf wrapping paper and tied with a huge red bow. Oh my, Monte had gone all out.

"What is it?" Nikki asked on the other end of the phone.

"Don't know yet, girl, but it's heavy. Thank you, Antoine. Would you like to come in?" I asked.

"No, ma'am, I'll wait in the car until you're ready. Take your time and enjoy your gift."

"Will you quit with the pleasantries and open the damn gift already!" Nikki blurted out.

"Okay, okay, I'm opening it. It's wrapped up so pretty, I don't want to mess it up."

"Open the goddamn gift, Nina." I could tell she was getting testy.

I dropped to my knees in the middle of my living room floor and began to rip that paper to shreds. Such a waste. Underneath the wrapping paper was a huge box. It was almost the size of Ariel, and it was bulging at the seams. After playing tug-of-war with the taped edges, I lifted the top off the box and made my way through the tissue paper.

"Oh my God, Nina! I could have driven over there to open it my damn self by now!" Nikki chimed in.

I sat back in amazement, trying to find the words, once I had dug through all of the tissue paper and had my hands on the actual gift.

"Heelo! Nina, what's going on? Did you get it open yet?"

"Yeah, Nikki, it's open. I . . . I think it's a mink coat," I stuttered.

"You think? Well, dammit, why don't you know? Pick it up and see! If it is, somebody has been withholding information, because I know that boy ain't get you a mink coat without even samplin' the goods."

"Hold on, Nikki." I had to put the phone down so I could appraise this coat for myself. Putting the phone on the floor, beside me, I could hear Nikki protesting loudly about having to wait.

I stood with the coat in my hand and lifted it in front of me; it was heavy. The coat was actually a jacket, and once I laid it on the couch and unzipped it, searching for some confirmation, there it was. I read the tag. Yep, it was a bona fide mink. Damn, this brother was really trying to step up his game, I guessed. I slipped into the jacket to see how it fit. Perfect. The jacket was a black onyx high-collared mink, cinched at the waist. It fell just about to my hips. It was fly, but I couldn't believe he had taken it there. I picked up the phone to see if Nikki was still on the line.

"Hey, girl, it's the bomb. That's all I can say." I was shocked and ecstatic all at the same time.

"Nina, are you still maintaining that Monte is not someone you are serious about? I mean, a fuckin' mink? I need to know what kind of soap you washing that pussy with so I can run out and buy some, because a mink coat is like a 'been together, about to get married' gift, not no damn we just kickin' it for a hot second present."

"Trust me, Nick. We just kickin' it, unless he knows something that I don't know . . . Anyway, we'll talk tonight, okay? I have a couple of things I need to do before we hook up."

"All right, chick. It's cool, but I'll be sure to get an update tonight. Holla."

I called Rahmel and got clearance to come pick Miles and Ariel up for a hot second. Miles loved cars, and I could not enjoy this moment fully without sharing it with him. I had Antoine stop in front of Rahmel's house, and I ran in to get my kids. Mel's brother, Big Hakeem, answered the door.

"Happy birthday, sis. Gimme some love. You looking good, girl." After a brief hug, he looked me in the eyes and asked, "How you holding up? You need any work done at that house, gimme a ring, you hear? We're still fam. You know that, right?"

I loved Rahmel's family. That would never change. They had a bond that I had never enjoyed in my own household.

"I promise. I'm doing well, though. Really I am."

Miles and Ariel ran into the room, with their coats in hand.

"Hey, tell Mel we'll only be a second. I have a little surprise for the kiddies," I said.

Miles was absolutely in love with the limo. He inspected the front and sat in the driver's seat, thanks to

Antoine's understanding. Little Miles loved cars and could almost name any make and model that drove by on any given day. We took a ride around the block, stopped to get a quick snack at the corner store, and then made our way back to their dad's. They were full of questions.

"Mommy, how'd you get a limousine?" Miles asked.

"Well, my friends just thought it'd be nice for me to be queen for a day and got it for me. It will go back after tonight."

"Aww man, I thought it was ours to keep," said Miles. He was not happy to hear we wouldn't be chauffeured on the daily. Little Ariel was just enjoying it while it lasted. She was content with running the short distance from the backseat to the driver's window without being strapped in.

"I like limousines, Mommy. It's big in here," was all she had to add.

I pulled out my digital camera and asked Antoine to take a picture of the three of us inside the limo for posterity. As Antoine pulled back in front of Rahmel's to deposit the kids, Miles took one last look.

"Mommy, can you take a picture of the outside of the limo, too? Please, Mom?" asked Miles. He must have wanted proof that he had driven in luxury, if only for a minute.

"No problem, baby. You and Ari pose, and I will take a picture of the two of you," I said. After the picture, we headed toward the house.

"Bye, Mr. Antoine. Thank you for the ride!" Miles yelled back. Antoine responded with a wave. After another quick hug and kiss from my babies, we said our good-byes for the second time today. They were tickled pink to have ridden in a limo, and I loved taking the time out just to make them smile.

Antoine opened the door for me, and I slid into the back of the limo. I could get used to this, I thought to myself.

"Where to, Ms. Tracy?" he asked politely.

"Back to my house please, Antoine," I replied in a kind tone.

I took out my cell phone and proceeded to call Monte. I didn't want any more time to pass before I acknowledged my gift.

Monte picked up on the first ring and started in before I had a chance to say hello. "Hey, baby doll, I was starting to think you didn't like my gift."

"I love your gift, both of them. Thank you, baby," I replied.

"Now, I don't know if you noticed, but the inside of the coat has a little tear. You gon' need to get that patched up."

"Oh yeah? I didn't notice that." I know I sounded puzzled, so Monte went on to explain.

"Look, baby doll, I'm a street dude. An associate of mine owed me some money, so I excused his debt for your coat. Since it's hot, he removed the serial number from the inside, you know, to keep it on the low and make sure you don't have any problems with it, feel me?"

Well, that explained the reason I was presented with such an elaborate gift; a street debt had been paid with a fur coat that had been stolen from some establishment that traced its merchandise with serial numbers, which is customary. No biggie in my book. I would have been running around naked as a kid if my uncles hadn't kept a supply of stolen merchandise flowing through our crib.

I responded casually, "Hey, get it how you live, baby. I didn't need all that explanation. I grew up with some of the smoothest boosters in town. All I care about is the fact that you thought enough about me to put it on my back." Now that was the truth. I must have been high on the totem pole.

"That's my baby, right there. Now that's some real shit. I was thinking you might have been a little stuck-up about the situation, you know," Monte said.

"Yeah, well, I'm full of surprises," I said. "Now let me go get dolled up for you, big poppa. I'll see you later on. Thanks again, baby. I love my jacket."

"Your welcome, baby doll. I'll see you tonight," Monte replied.

By now Antoine had pulled up in front of my house and had opened up the limo door for my exit. I went into the house and headed straight to my room so that I could start getting dressed for my big night out.

Chapter Five

The Celebration

My crew and I arrived at the Piccadilly fashionably late but fly as ever. I had taken extra pains in getting dressed tonight, knowing that all eyes would be on me. Plus, I'd be sportin' my new coat, so I had to be on point. I was rockin' a black, backless top with no bra. That meant my titties gave a little jingle every time I moved, which was cool as long as they were still standing.

I poured myself into a pair of skintight PZI jeans that hugged every curve of my body. To top off my ensemble, I had Antoine drive me to Nordstrom on the way to Monica's house. I was singing "Happy Birthday" to myself on the way back to the limo because I had just snapped on a five-hundred-dollar pair of black knee-high leather boots that I had eyed for the last month. I had purchased my boots and slid them on, taking a look in the floor-length mirror, before I left the store. I had been waiting for them to go on sale, but fuck it. This was my day, and my new mink coat deserved to be complemented with an equally sexy pair of boots. I couldn't wait to see everybody's reaction to these babies, a combination of black leather and suede, with intricate stitching; I was sure to be the belle of the ball.

I got in the limo and proceeded to pick up my girls for a night of partying. I ended up with Monica, Nikki, Nikki's girl Sherry, and Jonnie. Our next stop was Tee's, and then it was on to the plantation to pick up a few chicks responsible for closing up the place at the end of the night. That included Katrina, Danielle, and my girl Robin. They were all pumped.

We cracked open the bar in the limo and asked Antoine to make a couple of swings around the block before we headed to the club. I wanted to walk in with a good buzz. Sherry had a ready supply of weed. They managed to pass the blunt she had rolled around three times to those who wanted to partake before Antoine lowered the window separating us from him and kindly said, "Ladies, I'd hate to have to explain the smell if I was to get stopped by the police for any reason. Do you mind?"

Of course, they didn't mind. They had gotten just enough hits, coupled with a few drinks, to be well on their way to feeling good. I, on the other hand, had decided not to smoke tonight. I, in fact, insisted that they open the windows despite the cold air. They were not going to have smoke all up in my hairdo or my new jacket.

After everybody was finished drinking and the late-night crew put the finishing touches on freshening up their make-up, we finally headed toward the party. Antoine, being gracious as ever, opened the limo doors in grand fashion as we stepped out on the scene like there was a red carpet awaiting us.

I unzipped my mink jacket before stepping out, and Monica sneered, "Bitch, you lucked up on that. I been dating hustlers for the past ten years, and nary a one of 'em bought me no fucking mink. Cheap-ass sons of bitches."

I knew it was going to be a thin line between her loving and hating the fact that I was rocking this puppy. But if I knew Monica, it wouldn't be long before she charged one for herself.

Walking into the Piccadilly was like entering into one of them damn sweet sixteen shows on MTV. The setup wasn't elaborate, but my peeps were in full effect. I was getting love from everywhere. My ghetto-ass cousins had snuck my little sister, Kayla, in with a fake ID. She was grinning, ear to ear, like she had gotten away with murder. My little sis was at the age where we could really relate again, and I decided that I was going to do my best to be the mentor she needed.

I was getting much love from the job front, more than I ever even knew existed. All of my coworkers were on the scene. The word must have gotten around quick, because everybody from accounting and sales, and even a few of our cafeteria workers, were in effect. Around every corner, there was a familiar face: folks from my old neighborhood, my girls, and two fixtures from Monica's Monday night bowling league, one of which happened to be my sexy ass trainer, Dante and his sidekick Kevin.

I made my way over to greet Dante. "Well, look what the cat dragged in. I'm glad to see you," I said.

Dante always looked so damn clean-cut, like a

freaking rich frat boy, and was sporting a perfect low-cut fro, straight white teeth, and a body for life. He was dressed up like a business man. I wanted to rip the buttons off his shirt and eat him up.

"Hey Nina. Happy birthday, girl. What you drinking on?" Dante asked, giving me a birthday hug, which I savored a moment longer than I needed to.

"The usual," I responded, turning my attention to Kevin. "What's up, old man? Thank you for coming."

"My pleasure, little mama. Thanks for inviting us. We thought we were only honored to see you on Monday nights," Kevin said, referring to our typical Monday night gathering after the bowling league. "But this is love."

"You know better than that," I admonished.

Nikki passed by me long enough to hand me a drink, then kept it moving. She was on a mission, sporting a cowboy hat, leather coat, and some fly-ass cowboy boots. She was making sure that she didn't go unnoticed.

"Now, Ms. Tracy, go easy tonight. You know drinking will fuck up your workout and make you gain weight," Dante said to me. "Try to put a limit on your drinking, or I'm going to have to charge extra to keep that body in tip-top shape."

"Oh really? How much extra?" I asked. "My body could use some extra attention." Dante looked flustered, but he didn't take the bait.

His sidekick spoke up for him. "What kind of workout sessions do y'all be doing? Maybe I need to sweat a little." Kevin laughed like he had just said the punch line to a hilarious joke. I rolled my eyes and focused back on Dante.

"Dante McGowan, you better get on my wavelength

real soon, before this boat sails away." Putting my hand on my shapely hip, I added, "Now enjoy yourself tonight, and think about what I said."

I turned to leave without looking back. My exit was right on time. I could see Monte, his brother Marcus, and their boy Paris heading into the room. I acted as if I didn't have a clue that Monte had stepped in the building. Monte walked in like the party was going to stop to acknowledge his presence, but it wasn't about him. Not tonight. It was all about me! I had seen my uncles spoil their bitches and then expect them to play their position in order to stay in their good graces. Fuck that! Not I.

I made my way over to the party table, grabbed a couple of the chicken wings, which one of my cousins had cooked, a heap of mac and cheese, and few celery sticks. I hopped on a bar stool next to Monica and jumped right into a make-believe conversation.

"Bitch, what are you doing? You see your man done just stepped into the room?" Monica asked.

"Yeah, I see him. He'll make his way over here. I'm not going to bow down to him just because he bought a coat that probably didn't cost him a penny. You know it's hot, right? So don't get your panties in a bunch over nothing." I commenced eating my mac and cheese, effectively averting my eyes from the corner of the room Monte was in.

"Bitch, umm, so what. A mink coat is a mink coat, so long as it's yours. Why you playing him so tough? Are all brothers going to have to answer for Rahmel's bullshit?"

"Aye! That's enough! Don't you go there, not tonight." I said.

"Look, I like Monte. It's just game recognizes game, and I ain't about to be nobody's obedient-ass trophy bitch. Been there, done that. Plus, don't let his size fool you. He looks all right, but his dick is about this big. . . ." I held up my hand and used my thumb and forefinger to demonstrate the length of Monte's dick.

Monica's laugh was so loud, the rafters shook. "Girl, you are lying to me! When did you make this discovery?" Before I could answer, she added, "Go ahead. Ignore his big ass. As soon as his well runs dry, he won't do you no good, anyway. A short dick man can't quench your thirst." Monica was still giggling when Monte approached. I nudged her to stop. It was one thing to discuss a man's size, but it was downright rude to laugh at his shortcomings in his face.

"Hey, baby, I'm glad you could make it." I said as I got up from my bar stool and wrapped my arms around his massive shoulders. I planted a small peck on his cheek.

"Is that all the thanks I get?" said Monte. He looked disappointed. I knew I was right about his ass. He wanted to make shit all about him. He expected something for his gift, but there was a time and place for everything. This was neither the time nor the place.

"That's all for right now, Poppa," I said. "You know how I am about public displays of affection." I winked my eye and added, "But I have a big surprise for you later."

I could tell by the look on his face that he got my drift. I proceeded to greet everybody and make introductions. Monica immediately caught the eye of

Paris, and she commenced making him a plate like they had already been fucking. Nikki passed by long enough to say hey to the man that had been keeping a smile on her girl's face and a mink on her back. Then she kept it moving, but not before Marcus tried to holler at her. She fed him a few small lines, but too much was going on for me to watch for progress. But I knew Nikki would probably never hook up with him. He wasn't her style, too young.

The night was flying by me as I sat in the middle of a conversation with a few white girls from our operations department. I heard the Stevie Wonder rendition of "Happy Birthday" heading my way. To my surprise, there were my girls, Monica, Nikki, and Tee, along with Kayla and a host of others working their way through the club with a huge birthday cake, complete with lit candles. As soon as the cake landed on the table in front of me, I know my face must have turned three shades of red. The little white girls thought it was hilarious. I was relieved about that. I did not want to end up in Human Resources because my girls had presented me with a birthday cake that depicted a naked black man touting a humongous dick, with words coming out his mouth that read, "It's all for you. Baby! Happy Birthday Nina!"

I was happy to hear one of the little white girls exclaim, "Cut the cake, Nina! I hope it's chocolate, just like him."

Horny little bitches, I thought to myself. I discovered that after a few drinks, they sure weren't the little uptight princesses they presented themselves to be at work. For that, I was glad, because tonight was going to be off the chain. I made a wish and cut the cake right down the middle. Nobody was going to eat that big chocolate dick but me.

I must have gotten a little too loose for Monte, because in the middle of a picture-taking session, he snatched me up by my arm like he had ownership papers. I had just tooted my ass out while one of my girls smacked it. I guess this was the shit Monica was complaining about. Oh well, she'd have to get over it, but Monte wasn't so quick to do so.

"Come on, baby doll," he said. "I know it's your birthday, but you doing too much. Get yourself together so we can slide outta her. The limo is still waiting outside." Monte had the nerve to be pulling rank on me.

Okay, it's cool, I thought to myself. He had represented. Plus, I had downed more drinks than I could handle. I knew I was getting more buzzed than I should have when I started leaving drinks on the tables as soon as they were passed to me. Leaving drinks was a no-no unless you were on the verge of being a sloppy drunk. Wanting to maintain my composure, I decided to bow out gracefully.

I made sure my chicks had a ride back to the crib. Since everybody pretty much knew everybody, that was no big deal. It was easy for them to all cop a ride. I pulled my little sister to the side and asked, "How are you getting home?"

Kayla scoffed at my question. "Oh my God, Nina, I'm nineteen! I'm driving myself, and no, before you ask, I haven't had a lick to drink. It was too much fun taking notes on what everybody else was doing." She crossed her arms like she had made her point.

"Okay, now I don't want no mess, so come on. If I'm leaving, you're leaving." I knew she wanted to protest, especially if I looked as buzzed as I felt. But to hell with that. I was still big sis.

Monica was waiting her turn to get a word in edgewise. "Gimme some love, birthday girl."

We hugged like there was no tomorrow. Monica had been my foundation over the past year. Where would I be without her?

"You made it another year on this earth, and most importantly, you made it on your own, Nina. I'm proud of you." Monica leaned back and placed her hands on my shoulders, looking at me through beer goggles. I could still see the love in her eyes. "Now, are you about to give up the goods to Little Bo Peep?"

I tried to contain my laughter, with Monte being only a few steps away, but it was just too hard. We collapsed back into each other's arms and cracked up.

"Monica, okay. Well, let me explain. Maybe I overexaggerated when I showed you how small it is. It's average. I can make it work. I guess it's just like fucking the same average-ass dick you been fucking. I wanted him to be a ManDingo or something close to it." I wasn't making excuses, really I wasn't. An average pipe was okay as long as the owner worked it right. I thought about it and added, "I automatically assumed that it would be just as big as he is—"

"Girl, please, don't even play that game with yourself. Remember little skinny-ass Larry I used to fuck with? His dick was so big, I was light weight scared of it for a minute there. Don't believe the hype. These little brothers will fool you."

"I'll be sure to keep that in mind. Now let me go before I get my eye blackened. Monte's getting impatient. Love you, girl." I gave Monica another quick hug and joined Monte by the door.

"Come on now, baby. You done worked the room enough for tonight. It's time to go," Monte insisted.

He was right; I had worked the four corners. I grabbed hold of his arm, and we turned and walked arm in arm to the limo.

Antoine, always the gentleman, leaped out of the limo and stood to greet us, opening the door as he asked, "Did you enjoy yourself, Ms. Tracy?"

"I had a ball. Thanks for asking," I replied, climbing into the warm confines of the heated cabin. Before I sat down good, Monte was by my side. This was the moment of truth. He was expecting a pound of pussy, and I was aiming, to give it to him.

"You look so good to me, baby. I couldn't keep my eyes off you all night," said Monte. "All the men in the room were eyeing you, too, but you already know that, don't you?" I was engulfed in his big arms.

Shaking my head, I answered, "I hadn't noticed."

"Liar," was Monte's response. His hands glided along the curves of my body. I unzipped my coat to offer him full access to the treasures hidden beneath. Monte had been patient enough. Now it would be all about him.

Breaking free of the grip Monte had on me, I crawled out of his reach long enough to take off every article of clothing that was hindering him from properly seducing me. In turn, Monte did the same, removing his clothes without missing a beat. He soaked in every inch of me. I could only hope his lips would blaze the same path his eyes had just explored. Once undressed, Monte moved toward me like a hungry lion on the prowl.

He pulled me to him with one rock-hard arm. The heat of his body surrounded my naked flesh, and I clung to the warmth of him. Monte's mouth was like a heat seeker finding and tasting every sensitive spot on my body. My body arched to meet his, begging him without words to feed my need for satisfaction.

I spread my thighs and reached for him, and to my sheer delight, he lowered his head to the melting pot of desire that was awaiting him. Monte's tongue touched every fiber of my being and introduced me to a world of pleasure that had been somewhat foreign until now. Having never been sucked to orgasm, it was hard to wrap my mind around the sensations that were sending shock waves through my body. With my hands, I grabbed hold of Monte's shoulders for dear life. I was searching for a release from the flaming lava of heat that was building inside of me. Monte's tongue was taking me on a roller-coaster ride of ecstasy, and my passion soared to unimaginable levels, until finally the volcano erupted, and I was consumed by the heat.

On my way back to earth, I could feel Monte's body surround me, and in one swift thrust, he entered me. Realizing that I had been too dazed to make sure he had strapped up, I reached for his swollen member and felt the thin rubber veil, which was securely in place.

"Relax, baby doll. I got you. I got you," Monte assured me.

Relax I did. The first few strokes felt like heaven. My tight walls clung to him, and he dove harder and deeper into the caverns of my walls.

Monte's lips searched out mine, and his powerful thrusts came harder and faster, diving deeper and deeper into sensitive flesh. I raised my hips to meet his thrusts and watched with pleasure as he soared on the waves of passion to find his own release.

Afterwards, we lay together, basking in the moment. Monte wasn't so bad, I thought to myself. As long as that tongue stayed tuned up, he had a buddy for life.

Chapter Six

After The Party
It's The After Party

I must've looked like a fish out of water, and I couldn't believe that Monte had deposited me in the middle of the projects, smack-dab in the mix of his aunt Peg's first-of-the-month fish fry and card party. When Monte had first called me up and told me to get dressed because he wanted to take me somewhere, I had been under the false impression that this was going to be another one of our grand excursions, so I was dressed to the nines.

Donning the mink coat that Monte had presented me as a pre-birthday present, I was prepared to be shown off, but most definitely not in the projects. Now, I came from less than humble beginnings and I was no neat freak, but Aunt Peg didn't have the same standard of living I was accustomed to, and the folks up in her place were gawking at me like I had walked in the room with a Halloween costume on in the middle of their Fourth of July cookout.

Aunt Peg had a full-fledged bootleg spot going on in the basement of her project townhome. There were six plastic card tables arranged around the room, complete with dollar store Tupperware bowls in the middle to hold the bets until all the hands were played. And the entire family played a part in the running of the illegitimate business, from Peg's daughters, who served as hood gaming officials, to a couple of male family members, including Monte's fine-ass little brother, Marcus, who served as makeshift security guards.

So there I sat, venting my frustration in the rotation of my stiletto-encased foot. I sat in a corner, burning up with my mink coat on and my Gucci handbag wrapped around my wrist. I was not about to take my coat off and make Monte think I was getting comfortable up in that muthafucka. I was ready to go! This ghetto calamity of a card party was just the type of hood shit that some young hoodlums would run up in and rob, and I'd be damned if I wasn't going to be ready to head for the door at the first sound of some bullshit.

If you haven't caught my drift by now, I was pissed the fuck off! If Monte only knew how close he was to being labeled a rat bastard for pulling a stunt like this. He could have easily enlightened a sistah on his intentions with this date and told me to keep the shit casual. I mean, it wasn't the fact that I was in the projects; it was the fact that my attire was way too over the top for the environment in which I found myself. Like Julia Roberts suggests in the movie *Pretty Woman*, don't dress me up like a debutante and then tell people I'm a hooker. Let my dress be appropriate for the occasion, and then a bitch will be more comfortable.

Monte could tell my ass was on fire. But since he had gotten a little pussy from me already, he must have felt like his foot was in the door enough that he could stop frontin' on all of those elaborate type dates and start keeping the shit real. And giving me the mink might have helped, too, but fuck him. I wanted some attention! I wanted to be seen that night. I was looking too fly to be sitting in somebody's goddamn Section 8 town-house basement.

But there I sat, fuming, sweat running down my back, until Aunt Peg's bucktoothed daughter, Nay-Nay, decided to patronize the uppity-looking bitch in the corner.

"Hey, what's your name again?" she asked me.

I did my best to feign a smile. "Nina," I said politely.

"Good to know you, Ms. Nina. You want a drink?"

Yes, Lord, salvation, I thought. "Please . . . if you don't mind." Of course, she didn't mind. That appeared to be her sole duty. I ordered my usual, Tangqueray, grapefruit, and a splash of cranberry. Nay-Nay took my order and sauntered her bony, bucktoothed ass through the maze of tables crowding the basement and up the stairs, grinning all the way.

Monte had the audacity to finally try and pay me some attention after he had been paying most of his attention to the card game at hand.

"Hey, baby, unzip your coat. We're going to be here awhile," he said, looking over his shoulder like I was a damn afterthought. I wanted to stab him in his back for having me sitting back there, sweating like a whore in church.

Okay, Nina, stop pouting, and act like you've been halfway raised, I told myself. Taking a few quick breaths, I comforted myself with the fact that I could sit back here and drink until one of two things happened. Either I was going to get drunk enough to not give a damn that I was looking like a mink-wearing project chick, or by drinking Tang in the midst of my frustration, I was going to show my ass to the point that Monte had no choice but to escort me out of that bitch. Either way, I was going to act like a fucking lady, instead of pouting like little Ariel for not getting my way.

Right on time, here came Nay-Nay's narrow ass, weaving through tables, with my drink in hand. I could tell by the color of it that she had made it to my liking. "Here you go, Ms. Nina. That will be two dollars," she said, extending her hand to receive her money.

My back got straight for a second when I realized that Nay-Nay's hospitality was nothing more than a hustle to get some rent money. I reached into my purse to make a donation. *Shit, they must need it more than me,* I thought to myself.

Before I could grab my wallet, Monte shouted, "I got it, Nay!" and handed her a twenty-dollar bill. "Keep 'em coming, girl. My baby likes to get her drink on," he added.

Damn skippy, I thought to myself. At only two dollars a pop, how black of him to show that he cared. Monte ordered a double for himself and continued to play his card game.

Three drinks into the card game, and I think I

began to loosen up. Monte had switched tables and was in the middle of a hand of blackjack. I was seated against the wall, facing him, and the gin was doing wonders to improve my mood. As the old saying goes, "Gin will make you sin. If you don't believe me, go back the next day and try it again."

I was preparing to test the saying for myself. The seam of my jeans became a major distraction, and the more my eyes wandered over the perfect frame of Marcus's young body, the more my clit worried the seam of my Baby Phat jeans. I sipped my drink and tried my best to pretend the card game had my attention; all the while I was looking at Marcus from under my lashes.

As the game went on, and I allowed myself to settle into the fact that I could fuck that baby with no hesitation, I clenched my thighs and ground with no shame. I caught Monte's eyes and could tell the lust in mine was written all over my face. I raised my hand and gave him the sign to wrap it up.

Monte mouthed the words, "Are you ready to go?" and in return I licked my glossy lips slowly, pausing long enough to bite my bottom lip, like I was going to tear him apart.

Monte threw in his hand. "I'm out," he told them and stood to go.

I liked that in him. *Act like you know, nigga. It's about time,* I thought. Standing to leave, I said my good-byes and nice to meet yous, as if I was even going to try to remember everybody's name. I stood by the steps, waiting for Monte to make his rounds with his fam and took one last glance at Marcus, who was staring me dead in the face. I smiled politely; he smiled back.

Nina Tracy, get it together, I screamed to myself. Just as Monte turned to leave, I began my ascent up the steps, slowly, making sure Monte didn't miss one sway or the way my jeans were cupping my cheeks.

Once Monte and I made our way to the car, the shit was on. He hadn't even pulled out of the parking space before I began to stroke his dick, which hardened in my hands.

"Damn, girl, what you trying to do?" he asked.

"If I have to say it, then something's wrong with this picture," I told him.

"Do your thang then, baby girl," he said as he placed his hand on the back of my head.

"Wait a minute," I told him as I dug down in my purse and pulled out my lip gloss. "I gotta make this pretty." I took out my lip gloss and began to polish my lips. After a couple of loud puckers, I placed the lip gloss back into my purse and turned to face Monte. "Now where were we?"

"If I have to say it, then something's wrong with this picture," he replied and winked, hitting me with my own words.

"You wanna be a smart-ass, huh? Then take this." I proceeded to unzip his Sean John jeans and pull his throbbing dick out of his pants through the slit in his boxers. I then began my David Copperfield disappearing act, forcing his muscle to vanish deep in my throat.

"Oh, shit," he murmured and squirmed, gripping

the steering wheel with his hands the same way I was gripping his dick with my lips. "Do that shit."

It was the weirdest thing; I seemed to get off better sucking Monte's dick and making him cum than putting in work trying to make my pussy cum. I don't know, but there was just something erotic about the way he responded to the flipping and thrashing of my tongue on his centerpiece.

Up and down, I bobbed my head as I slurped on his stick like it was a lollipop. "Ummm," I began to hum, giving an added sensation, which had this nigga damn near running red lights.

I could feel his hand pressing the back of my head, guiding me up and down. We were in a constant rhythm. We were in sync.

"Oh, shit," he said and tensed up.

I looked up and smiled a knotty smile. I loved fucking him with my teeth every now and then. "My bad," I lied and then went back to the business at hand.

I caressed his manhood with my hand while I manipulated the tip of his dick with my tongue, which drove him insane. Flick, flick, flicker, I plucked at him like a guitarist would his guitar. I could feel his muscle getting tighter and tighter. I knew he was about to bust. Just then I felt the car slowing down. I knew we were about to come to a stop. That was when I began to suck fast and hard. Hard and fast.

Monte turned up the radio, and a Snoop Dogg song blared in my ear. It was befitting of the moment. Plus, I got a tingle out of the pimp shit Snoop was spitting into the atmosphere.

I paused for a quick second and looked Monte in the eyes. "Are you going to be able to keep your mind on the road while I'm sucking your dick?"

"Hell yeah. I'm a grown-assed man, baby doll. Now get back to business."

I couldn't help but notice our change in speed, and I realized that we had entered the freeway. I got turned on by the thought of some hard-up truck driver looking down on me while I sucked Monte's dick. Monte reached his hand inside my jeans, grabbing a handful of ass. I unbuttoned my jeans and slipped them down over my ass. If the sight of me giving head didn't catch the attention of a fellow driver, the sight of my ass in the air would definitely get their attention.

"Oh, damn! Oh shit! Baby, whoa," Monte said. "Hold up."

Monte jerked his dick out of my mouth like a punk. I looked around to see that we hadn't driven far from the exit of the freeway, and Lord help me, we were parked right in front of the Trinity Baptist Church.

"What's the matter?" I asked, confused as to why we had stopped.

"Nothing. As a matter of fact, everything is right." He kissed me on my lips.

"Then why are we stopped?"

"Because," was all Monte said as he reached for my waist and pulled me to him. "Take off those jeans. I wanna feel that pussy on my dick, baby."

That was fine by me, so I jumped out of my jeans and climbed onto Monte's dick without hesitation.

Monte reached for my hips and plunged into the depths of my wetness. I rode him something fierce, grinding my clit against his pelvis.

"I want to see you, baby. Take off your shirt. Pull that shit off," said Monte.

With one quick tug, my shirt was over my head. Monte pushed my bra straps off my shoulders and tickled my nipples with his tongue. The pressure was building. When he brought his mouth from my nipples and back to my lips, I could feel myself getting weak. We had found our rhythm. My body was in flames, and the fire was being fed with every thrust of my hips.

Monte tried to stop the rotation of my hips; knowing he was about to bust, I kept working them with a vengeance. "Fuck that," I said. "Give it to me."

I was about to make this nigga cum. The dance I was performing on his pipe would have brought a weaker man to his knees, but Monte was no ordinary man. His mission was to please, but I was on a mission to prove that tonight he was the weakest link.

The next thing I knew, there was an explosion in my eardrums as Monte yelled his release for the whole neighborhood to hear. A loud, blaring noise, which was Monte pushing down on the horn as he came, probably woke the entire neighborhood.

"Mmmm, hmmm," I moaned, taking it all in as he freaked out over the sheer feeling of ecstasy. "Go ahead. Say it," I hinted.

"Whatever you want, baby. What do you need to hear?" Monte asked.

"Tell me if it was as good as you made it seem." I wrapped my scantily clothed body around Monte for warmth. The chill was starting to seep in now that the sex had come to a halt.

"It was all that, baby doll. I put that on everythang." Monte pulled the seat forward and proceeded to drive.

"Hold up, baby. Let me get myself together," I

pleaded. Shit, I was still sitting on this nigga's dick, naked as the day I was born.

"Shhh, baby doll. Stop moving! I don't want you to go nowhere. I like you just the way you are, sitting on my dick."

"Monte, come on now. What about the police?" It was fun while it lasted, but now that it was over, I wasn't trying to get a public indecency charge.

"Fuck the police. I got them in my back pocket," Monte explained.

Well, in that case, show me what you have in mind, I thought to myself.

Monte was growing inside of me again, and as we rode down side streets and stopped at red lights, I couldn't help but wonder if the folks in the cars next to us were wondering if they were drunk or if their eyes were just simply deceiving them.

Monte stopped every so often to get a little taste of my offerings. I sucked on his ear and planted a garden of kisses on his neck and shoulders. Before long, we had arrived at my house.

"Come on. Let's get in the house. You was talking too much shit in the car," said Monte. He was on a mission.

I snatched up my jeans, which were dangling from one ankle, slipped into my jacket, and jumped out the car. Monte pulled up his jeans and lifted me out of the car like a sack of potatoes.

"What you rushing for? This pussy ain't going nowhere," I teased.

"Uh-huh, damn right it ain't," was his simple reply.

Monte took my keys and opened the front door, kicking it shut with his booted foot. He walked up the steps two at a time, as if my big ass was light as a feather.

Laying me on the bed, he insisted, "Take that shit off, and hurry up."

I liked the aggressive side of Monte, and I did as I was told. I opened my legs, welcoming him inside of me. He climbed on the bed, but he had a different goal in mind.

Grabbing me by my thighs, he lowered his head to the peach fuzz between my thick thighs. I wanted to cry foul. That boy knew his mouth was a lethal weapon. He was trying to get at me by any means necessary for pulling that nut outta him earlier. The last thing I heard before he used his tongue to send me off into ecstasy was, "Payback is a bitch."

Chapter Seven

That's What Friends Are For

I put in a twelve-hour workday while my babies were over at their dad's, the rat bastard, something I never called him in front of the children.

I picked up the phone to hear their voices before they went to bed for the night. At the end of our phone call, my five-year-old, Miles, made me promise to call 991 if any monsters came while they were at their daddy's. I made a promise to get a knife and do exactly as he told me if any monsters should come.

I smiled to myself at Miles's brave front. He was trying his best to be a big boy for Mommy, but the divorce hadn't set well with either of the kids.

I had agreed to meet with Monica and some friends after work at a local bar to blow off some steam. I stopped home long enough to freshen up and throw on some jeans. Lord knows, a quick shower was past due after the day I had. Sometimes, I swear, kissing up to clients, attending meetings, and arranging lunch dates made my work in the field of advertising seem like a day of welding steel.

The Back Room was a local bar that can be summed up in four words: hole in the wall. This was the designated meeting spot where we gathered after a couple of my peeps' weekly bowling league games.

I am not sure what brought us to this spot every week; it could be that the drinks were off the hook and the folks were genuine. The Back Room was small and consisted of a large bar that took up the center of the room, with several small tables scattered around the perimeter. I walked in to see that pretty much nothing had changed since the last visit.

There was a small dance floor, which overflowed with bodies on Friday nights, but tonight it was bare except for an older gentleman in his mid- to late sixties who appeared to be reliving his glory years.

When I entered the club, Monica waved me back to where they were seated, which was in a back corner, at one of the many square tables that were positioned around the room. I stopped at the bar first and ordered my usual drink: Tanqueray with cranberry and a splash of grapefruit. I then made my way to the back.

Assembled around the table was our usual group: Monica, Tricia, Dante, and his boy Kevin. Both Kevin and Dante had been buddies with my girls for years. Monica and Kevin had had a brief fling, nothing serious, but I was under the impression that they got together every now and then to get each other off. Other than that, we were just a group of friends with a pastime of drinking and cracking on each other every chance we got.

The Old G on the dance floor was the unknowing butt of our jokes as his antics persisted and the drinks kicked us into overdrive. Tonight was a little different, though. For some strange reason, this cold night in February had a certain vibe that seemed to be warming us all up.

As I sat back and casually sipped my gin and juice, I caught Dante staring unashamedly at my breasts. I smiled and licked my lips casually.

"Damn, Nina, I don't want to offend you, but have I ever told you how good you look?" Dante said. I guessed the liquor was giving him courage. "I have to pat myself on the back for some of that there, girl. My sessions done turned a work of art into a masterpiece."

Dante had always been a bit of a show-off, but at this moment, he seemed a little more tame compared to how he normally acted. I leaned back in my chair and arched my back discreetly, giving him more of a view. I carried on as if I was unaffected by his words. Inside, a fire began at my thighs and spread like wildfire to the rest of my body.

When Dante and I would meet up for my training sessions, he would exhibit complete and utter professionalism. I would be up in the gym, trying my best to look like Serena Williams, and he would never so much as blink an eye. Now here he was, for the first time ever, acknowledging what I was working with.

I did my best to appear unfazed by his comment. "Thank you, dear heart," I replied as I sipped another drink without breaking our eye contact. I knew it. I could tell that this was my moment to make my move on Dante, and I had the full intention of letting it be known.

"Let's toast to the masterpiece you've created" I said. "Your attention in the gym has molded me in more ways than one. I can only hope we're blessed with many more sweat sessions in the months to come."

I held Dante's gaze while our glasses touched. "Read between the lines already!" I screamed to myself. Monica interrupted our moment as she yelled drunkenly, "Aye, y'all. Let's do something different tonight! I'm tired of the damn Back Room!"

Clearly, I needed to catch up fast on the drinking, because they were a good three drinks ahead of me according to Monica's behavior.

"There's a titty bar up the street," Kevin said, with a snakish grin.

Tricia, who had been quiet and just enjoying her drink up until now, chimed in. "I can't go in a strip club, boy, please! My husband is not having that."

Tricia was quiet and usually just there for the ride. She sat and laughed at our jokes but rarely made one of her own. Monica and I were determined to get her out of her shell, and after a few obscene suggestions from her girls, she smiled and buried her chin in her chest. "Okay, I'll go, but no one ever speaks a word about this to anybody." We sealed the deal with a pinky promise and finished off our drinks, then headed out to our newest destination.

When we opened the door and emerged from the bar, the cold wind slapped our faces as if it knew we were about to misbehave. We all walked to our respective cars and pulled up along one another to map out the best way to the strip club.

"Don't be taking us to a strip club with a bunch of

tore-up babes!" I yelled to Kevin. "I only tip dime pieces," I continued, talking shit.

"Girl, I know every titty bar in town, and I only go to the ones with dubs. How about that?" he replied confidently and winked his eye for added assurance.

As soon as we mapped out our plan, Monica said her buzz had worn off from the smack in the face she had gotten from the cold wind. She suggested we go to her crib and do a couple of shots to get back in the zone so that we could have a more enjoyable time in the titty bar.

I knew my time was limited, and I had an early appointment the next day. Looking at the clock, I saw that it was already ten o'clock, so time was of the essence. I halfheartedly agreed to go back to Monica's place first, and then we all ended up driving the short distance to Monica's crib.

Monica's home was the equivalent of a female bachelor pad. Her home was strictly for partying and had all the necessary ingredients for us to accomplish our mission.

Several pieces of expensive art adorned her walls, and her furniture made one hesitate before having a seat. Monica took painstaking efforts to give the effect that she led a glamorous life. The creamy white carpet that ran through her town house was a good clue that she didn't have any kids.

Although Monica surrounded herself with expensive things, and the décor in her home reflected it, when I went to her refrigerator to grab a snack, I found it completely bare, with the exception of condiments, beer, and juice. What she lacked in substance, she made up for with plenty of alcohol.

I grabbed the ingredients to make an apple martini and went to work. Monica soon joined me, bitching about my option to sip on martinis rather than down tequila. I knew all too well that if tequila got a hold on me, I would surely forget about my appointment the next day.

We settled in Monica's cozy den, a few steps down from her upper level. Monica went to the radio and turned on some teenybopper song that gave explicit instructions on how to shake your ass. It only took a couple of shots for my girl to be back to where she was twenty minutes prior.

Once the liquor started flowing and the music got good, an official dance off began—the girls against the guys. My ass had always been my asset, so I commenced shaking it. All the while the once shy and reserved Tricia gave the men a glimpse of her well-endowed breasts. Monica and I shared knowing looks. Tequila did not discriminate, and once it had you, you were liable to step out of character.

The music was loud, and the drinks were plenty. Monica dimmed the lights to provide a little ambiance. I backed my thang up against Dante while Monica and Tricia closed in on Kevin.

"I'll be right back. Don't move," I said to Dante as I made my way up the few short steps to make a quick call to Monte before I got caught up. I was digging Monte, that was no lie, but I'd be lying if I said that Dante didn't have my undivided attention at this very moment.

"Hey, big boy did you miss me today?" I said into the phone receiver after dialing his phone number. I liked the way his voice lit up when he knew it was me.

"There's my baby," he said. "I was beginning to

wonder if you fell asleep at the plantation." I laughed at his reference to my job. "Where you at, baby? Sounds like you kicking it."

My back got straight for a second as I realized Monte was questioning me. "Over Monica's. We stopped by her crib to get a few drinks. I'll be outta here soon. I've got an early morning meeting," I replied.

"Oh well, now you know what they say. No time like the present. Take your ass home, Nina. I ain't a fan of house parties."

I was taken aback a little bit by the tone in Monte's voice. He had never come at me like that before, a taste of pussy must've had him feeling himself. I did like the fact that this brother was up in his chest over my actions, but at the same time, I didn't want him to get twisted, either. I was newly single and not about to settle back down anytime soon, or be on lock-down, for that matter.

I pacified Monte with assurances to get him off the phone. I made another drink for the road and made my way back down the steps. The mood had certainly changed. Monica had her drink in one hand and nothing but a pair of thongs on. Apparently, the strip club had moved to 1666 East Windsor Drive.

I continued down the steps, and I thought for sure my eyes were deceiving me. I looked in amazement as the shy, demure Tricia wiggled out of her jeans and bent over to present Dante with a look at her smooth brown ass, her pink thongs accentuating the color of her skin.

I must have looked just as dumbfounded as Dante and Kevin, having never had a show like this from our little virginal Tricia. *Well, hell,* I thought as I made my way down the stairs. *I ain't no damn party pooper.*

With that thought, I slid my jeans off, and not to be upstaged, I threw one leg over the end table and arched my back, giving them a healthy view of my golden ass in a pair of racy boy shorts. I knew from looking in the mirror and admiring my own reflection that the lacy edges were framing my booty cheeks like a picture in a frame. Dante's face was all I was concerned about, and his reaction was priceless.

My hair spilled over my face, and I pulled it back and smiled at Dante. "Do you like that?" I asked as I stared boldly at him, challenging him with my eyes. He shook his head wholeheartedly, and then the guys began a strip show of their own for the ladies.

We sat on the couch, with drinks in hand, and laughed at their antics as they imitated the show we had just given them. Kevin walked over to Monica and began gyrating in front of her. Kevin broke it down and was tipped with a kiss. One seemingly innocent kiss led to another, and it wasn't long before Kevin and Monica were on the verge of something serious. *Time to get a room,* I thought to myself. The next thing I knew, Tricia pulled off her top and unhooked her bra, presenting us with a view of her large brown breasts. I guess she figured she was going to get a piece of the action her damn self.

Tricia's breasts were huge and sat up proudly, with nipples like two gargantuan Hershey Kisses. I resisted the urge to touch one, feeling suddenly shy. What was going on here exactly? I thought to myself. The scene had changed too quickly.

I reached for my martini and took a swig. I watched as Dante reached for Tricia's breast, in awe, and grabbed a handful like he was collecting food to store away for the winter. He had no qualms about feeling those suckers out.

"When in Rome . . . ," I said under my breath. I wasn't about to let Tricia collect on the fantasies all by herself . . . my fantasies. I wanted to jump on her back and dig my claws in her, toss her to the floor, and tell her to take her married ass home to her man. There was no way in hell I was competing with her ass.

I took a few deep breaths and polished off my drink, rose to my feet, and joined Tricia with a striptease of my own. I walked around her, seductively stroking her brown skin. Then I turned my attention to Dante. Looking him in the eyes, I removed my shirt and stood before him in my Vicky's. His eyes traveled the length of my frame as I stood there, proudly letting him take it all in. Lord knows, I did not imagine it would go down between the two of us like this, but what the hell? I had waited for the opportunity to come, and here it was.

Monica disappeared from the room and came back and showered us with condoms. The silver wrappers glistened in the air, and we laughed at the enormity of what we had embarked on. The condoms meant what we had all admitted, without words, that we were about to fuck.

Grabbing a couple of condoms from the carpeted floor, Monica lay back on the love seat to oversee the scene unfolding before her. I saw her trying to let the situation unfold. That's when, Nina the Sex Diva took complete control, and without a second thought, I went over to my best friend and kissed her square on the lips. She returned the gesture by slipping me the tongue. She then looked up at me, as if to say, "That's what friends are for."

Behind me, I could hear delightful moans and turned to see shy Tricia with her legs in the air. Kevin was delving into her. His narrow ass was pale in comparison, and his thin frame seemed to be giving her all he had to offer. I turned to Monica and smiled. She had a sly smirk on her face and mumbled to me, "I knew that bitch wasn't no angel. She's a ho, just like the rest of us."

We shared a laugh, and I continued with the business at hand. I dipped my head to Monica's breasts and teasingly licked. I moaned with pleasure as I felt Dante behind me. His tongue made love to the small of my back and delivered wet kisses to my ass. I inhaled sharply as he entered me from behind.

He grabbed my hips and whispered, "I never thought in a million years that I'd have the chance to do this, so I'm going to tear your ass up."

I arched my back and presented him with all the pussy he could take.

"Work that shit," I said out loud. My hands were all over Monica, and the lust in her eyes was evident in the way she stared at us. Kevin carried himself away from the insult he had inflicted on Tricia, who was left panting as if she had lost a school-yard fight, and then bent over Monica and began planting sloppy kisses on her.

Dante smacked my ass as a signal for me to change positions. I lifted my body from Monica's and, once again, assumed the position. As I arched my back, I glanced at Tricia and motioned for her to join us. She seemed to hop the short distance between us and lay down while I sampled her ebony lips and chocolate breasts.

"I've never done this before," she whispered as she lay stiffly beside me.

In my mind, I laughed, and I hid the smile that was on my face in her large breasts. Tricia might not have actually done "it" before, but it had definitely been on her mind, just like it had been on my mind for so many years. We had played the fantasy of an orgy out in our minds so many times that when it actually came time for the fantasy to become a reality, we fell right into our roles.

I just couldn't help thinking that if Tricia's husband didn't approve of her just going to a strip club, then what in the world would he think about this?

Dante slowly circled inside me as he stared down at the delicious sight before him. We must have looked like a tasty treat, with Tricia's deep chocolate skin and my light caramel complexion combined. I allowed my lips and tongue to carefully explore her body while I received Dante from the back.

Kevin's and Monica's moans could be heard echoing throughout the room. The air was thick with lust, and I melted in the passion. A few minutes after emitting a high-pitched moan, Monica joined us on the floor and kissed Tricia seductively on the lips.

Dante insisted on seeing my face while he fucked me, so I turned over onto my back to oblige him. He thrust inside of me, and I met his thrust with equal enthusiasm. The next thing I knew, my sexual boundaries were put to the test.

I didn't have time to speak or protest. All I could comprehend was Monica's thick thighs crossing my face and blocking the candlelight from view. She had perched her pussy squarely over my face, and I didn't have time to think about how I felt about this. I admit that I somehow felt violated, but I ain't no sucker, and I wasn't about to punk out.

I let my tongue go to work the best way I knew how. Being a woman myself, it wasn't hard for me to figure out what to do. My lips and tongue beat to the same rhythm as hers. My body seemed to take over my mind, and I was carried away, licking Monica's pussy like a passionate kisser.

"Damn, Nina!" Monica gasped before she caught herself screaming a woman's name. Monica collapsed to the floor in pure pleasure, as if I had sucked everything up out of her.

Ummm, one down, one to go, I thought.

Noticing we had an onlooker, Dante knelt to my ear and declared, "I ain't finish with you yet, girl," as he rolled next to me.

His pipe still rock hard, he was a challenge I wasn't up for at the moment. I had more pertinent business to attend to.

I scurried up the steps, with assorted items of clothing in my hands. I entered the bathroom to see Kevin standing in front of the toilet, dick in hand, as if he was waiting for permission to pee. I jokingly smacked him on the ass.

"Stop playing, girl!" he yelled.

He leaned back and pissed casually, like I was one of his boys. I proceeded to turn on the water and splash around. He glanced down at me, and a crooked grin appeared on his face. "That was better than any titty or ass-shaking bar I ever went to," he said and laughed.

"I'll bet," I answered casually. I wiped the water

from my face and snatched up the mouthwash and began to gargle. Kevin thought the shit was just utterly hilarious.

"Now you know how we feel about going downtown," he joked.

I continued to gargle and chose to ignore the humor he found in my situation. We went back down the hall and entered the den. Everyone appeared to be relaxed and fully sedated, with the exception of Dante.

His erection was still in full force. He smiled and grabbed my hand, bringing me onto the love seat, next to him.

"I told you I was going to give it to you good now that I have you," he reminded me.

This man had my senses in an uproar. Monte catered to my every desire, from the just-because gifts to the spontaneous nights out on the town, but Dante moved my soul. I kissed him seductively, slowly savoring every second of the time I had. All the while I stroked and teased his hardness.

With the music still playing in the background, we barely noticed our audience. They were ready for a show, but I was in no mood to perform. As if he had read my mind, Dante whispered in my ear, "Let's go take this to the bedroom."

I was on my feet in an instant, and we ran up the steps like two newlyweds. Of course, Monica was in tow, pouting and protesting at the top of her intoxicated lungs. "Oh, hell no. This is my crib! I'm the only one fucking in that bed!"

Finally, she saw that her protests were falling on deaf ears as Dante and I made our way to her bedroom. Dante demanded I remove the rest of my clothes so he could have all of me. I obliged him by removing each remaining article of clothing piece by piece.

Before my bra could hit the floor, Dante scooped me onto the bed. He grabbed my hips, pulling me down to his face.

"That's what I'm talking about," I muttered to myself.

I arched my back and pressed my pussy into his face. He worked his tongue in ways I had never felt. I swear he was doing somersaults down there. My hands were in his hair, pulling his head into me, and I was working my hips to the beat of his tongue. I moaned and shook my head. I never wanted the feeling to stop.

"I need to feel you, baby," Dante said. He slowly ascended my body, still evoking pleasure with his lips. As he reentered my body, he growled as if he'd been away far too long. I allowed him only a moment to get reacquainted before I pushed him back and took control. Dante grabbed one of my breast and put my nipple in his mouth. I slowly circled my hips and allowed myself to dwell in the pleasure my body was experiencing.

I was in a greedy mood and wanted to show Dante what I was working with, so I pressed my hands into his chest, pushing him off of me, and then planted my feet on the bed and rode him like a jockey.

"Oh shit!" Dante exclaimed, awestruck by my change in tempo.

I rode that man like my life depended on it. I turned sideways and let him have it, letting my hips drop full force onto him. Turning completely around, I rode him backwards, only to find Kevin leaning over the bed, dick in hand.

"Damn man, y'all ain't playing!" Kevin said.

I could tell he wanted to play, too, but I was sticking with the good loving I was getting right here. I arched my back up and down powerfully, and Kevin smacked my ass, as if to say "Giddyup!"

Dante moaned loudly. In fact, I had never heard a man make so much noise in my life. It was a powerful feeling.

I heard Monica down the hall, yelling, "It ain't that damn good!" with envy in her voice.

I turned back around to face Dante. "Is it, baby?" I asked. "Is it that good?"

"Oh, hell yeah," Dante replied.

He put my nipple back in his mouth. I could see the smirk on his face as he accepted it.

"Now I'm ready," I whispered to him, with a gleam in my eyes, ready to take this thing to the next level . . . as if we could get any higher.

My back was covered with sweat, but I was going for broke. It had been so long—too long—since I had a fat dick between my legs. Dante grabbed all the ass his hands could hold and forced my hips up and down. My orgasm was powerful. Dante controlled my hips once it took over my entire body. I was breathless and soaked with sweat as I lay across his chest, breathing heavily.

Dante turned me over, put my legs over his arms, and prepared for his own release. It is no exaggeration when I say I have never heard a man yell like Dante did. At one point, I didn't know if the man was still cumming or if he had pulled a damn muscle and was in physical pain.

He carried on so much that Kevin, who at some point had left the room, came back in to see what the fuss was about. It did wonders for my ego, Kevin seeing Dante lying across me, grabbing the sheets, and me patting his back, like he was a newborn baby.

"What she do to you, boy?" Kevin said, with disgust in his voice. He got no reply from a speechless Dante.

We took our time getting dressed, admiring each other's bodies and taking a mental inventory of what had just occurred. Was this night actually real? Did everything that I thought went down really go down? Or was my mind fucking with me again? An aftershock suddenly flowed through my body as I quivered. Oh yeah. It was real.

I wasn't sure how or if this would change the nature of Dante and my relationship, but one thing was for sure, my crush had turned out to be just as good as my fantasies.

I took my time in the bathroom, getting myself situated. And although it crossed my mind, I didn't waste my time feeling guilty about Monte. He was a big boy and a hustler. As few and far between as our rendezvous were, I was pretty sure he had a bottom bitch that was making time for him and giving him the sexual intimacy I had yet to allow myself to succumb to with him. But hell, after tonight, I could succumb to anything.

I made my way into the den to see Monica seated on the couch, with her face screwed up, arms folded. "My neighbors are gon' think all that noise was me!" she yelled jokingly.

She dropped her show of anger and laughed hysterically. We all sat in the den and decided this was worth discussing over food.

"Where's Tricia?" I asked.

"Girl, you know she scooted her ass out of here as soon as the lights came on!" Kevin exclaimed. We all enjoyed a good laugh about how her "shy" ass hadn't hesitated to come up out of her clothes.

Once again, there we were, eating good food and discussing the change in events. We hollered when Dante walked in with a limp, like he had been seriously broken off.

"Now," Monica began in a tone that commanded attention, "don't be expecting no pussy every week, now shit. This right here was just letting off a little steam."

Kevin had a comeback "Shiiittt . . . if I had know y'all was down for that, I would have flipped the script on bowling night years ago. Girl, don't be trying to tease a brotha, then take it back!"

It was amazing to me how a simple change in plans had totally altered the scope of the relationships I'd had with the folks I had been around all my life. In an instant, I and my unsuspecting group of friends had crossed over into what seemed like the twilight zone.

Dante and I exchanged looks across the table. *What happens now?* I asked myself. I had taken a chance and had put myself out there with Dante. Now I wondered what he would think of me and of us. Not that there really was an us, but we definitely had built something of a relationship at the gym, hadn't we?

At Monica's insistence, we all agreed that this would not affect our friendships and would not be repeated. By repeated, Monica meant not only were we to keep our mouths shut, but also there would be no more sexcapades between us. I'm sure Dante and I made that promise with our fingers crossed, because if he wanted more sex from me, I was sure aiming to give it to him.

Chapter Eight

One On One

Dante and I were heading down the steps from the workout floor to the locker area, and just as he was wrapping up his motivational speech on how well I was doing, I made my move.

"So are we going to continue to meet up like this, with no mention of what went down the other night?" I asked him. Of course, he knew that I was referring to the orgy of sorts that had gone down at Monica's crib just a few days prior.

Since our party of five, I had had a couple personal training sessions with Dante, but it was back to business as usual. It was like that orgy had been forgotten. Like it hadn't really been us, but instead, had been a scene from the college anthem movie *Animal House*. After all, that's what we had all acted like that night: a bunch of inebriated college students on a faraway campus, who would one day go our separate ways, leaving the past behind. Of course, that wasn't the case for us. We were all full-fledged adults who knew just what the fuck we were doing. I stopped my trek and casually leaned against the wall leading into the women's locker room as I waited for his response.

"Shit, Nina," he said, taking a breath and shaking his head, as if he had been holding his breath, just waiting for the moment when I'd bring up our encounter. "Everything went down so quick that I didn't know what to make of it. The way I see it, everybody was a little out of their element, you know?"

"Uh-huh." I listened as he continued.

"We were all drinking and having a good time, so I figured I might insult you, that I might be overstepping my boundaries if I brought it up, seeing as how I never really saw you in that light. You know what I'm saying?"

Dante was grasping for words, but I was prepared to make it easy for him. "I hear what you're saying, and all I have to say to that is the only way you're going to insult me is by carrying on as if the sex wasn't as good for you as it was for me."

I cannot tell a lie. I may have been standing before him like I was the man, holding my crotch, with my chest out or some shit, but my stomach was doing flip-flops while I waited for his comeback. Thank goodness he didn't keep me waiting long.

"I haven't stopped thinking about you in that sense since that night. You coming in here and me training you like business as usual has been a mind trip for me."

Just then we heard the steps of someone heading our way towards the locker room. Dante had something else to say, but he didn't want to risk her hearing. So he leaned in closer, as if he had a secret on the tip of his tongue and it was only meant for my ears. "I haven't stopped wanting to feel you underneath me since you drove away."

Satisfaction, yes! Being an aggressive bitch wasn't just good for the workplace. "So, now that we're on the same page, do you think you can manage to make me sweat outside the gym?" I could tell by the surprised expression on his face that my boldness, which was not alcohol induced, shocked him. Hell, I was going for shock value, so I continued. "I got a few spots that need some target training, and while you're at it, a few stretches would do me some good."

Dante looked dumbfounded. "Tonight," he whispered, like he was gasping for air.

He was anxious. I liked that in him, so I decided to increase his anxiety level by making him wait.

"Tonight's a no-go," I told him. "Me and my kids are kicking it, but tomorrow, after I put their little behinds to sleep, you can stop by. How about that?"

Dante didn't need any time to think. "Sounds like a plan. I'll see you tomorrow night."

Tomorrow night was now here, and I felt like a virgin on prom night as I prepared myself for the unexpected. My stomach was churning, and I took deep, slow, steady breaths to settle my nerves. Dante was coming. And if all worked out as planned, he would be cumming.

It was about eleven o'clock when I saw the headlights of Dante's car enter my driveway. The kids had been sound asleep in their upstairs bedroom for over an hour by then.

I exited my bedroom and headed downstairs. I was in such a hurry that I skipped a step and almost fell and broke my leg.

"Get it together, Nina. You're a grown ass woman. Act your age, bitch," I said aloud.

For the first time in a very long time, I could feel the anticipation growing inside me. You know that feeling you get when you're young and your crush gives you a little attention? For some reason, Dante always gave me butterflies.

I made my way down the stairs and gave myself one last pep talk. "Man up," I told myself and then gave myself one last cursory glance in the living room mirror before I headed toward the door.

I'd never in all my years been such a slut. Rephrase that. An intentional slut on a mission to get fucked.

Two soft knocks hit the door. *Showtime,* I told myself.

I opened the door slowly and stood in the entrance, proudly displaying my wares. I was wearing black thigh boots with a lacy black thong and a barely there black bra. The cool winter air touching my skin was an afterthought. My nipples sprang to attention.

"I almost started without you," I said jokingly as I moved from the doorway to allow him entry into my abode.

"Ms. Tracy, what a pleasant surprise." Dante looked like a man that had his hole card pulled.

Once he entered, I shut the door behind him and turned to take his coat. I paused only for a second to inhale the scent of his cologne. Finally, there was a man in my house! Not taking anything from Monte, but he just didn't give the same thrill that I got from Dante.

Dante turned to me with a smile and a bottle of Tanqueray. "I brought your favorite."

"Thank you." I looked down at his dick. "And I see you brought me a bottle of Tanqueray, too."

He smiled. I could tell he liked the kind of slick shit that was sliding off of my tongue and into his ear.

I took the bottle and set it aside without a second thought. With my mind on one thing and one thing only, I pressed the length of my body against his. "I hope you brought *all* my favorites," I whispered as I pressed my lips against his.

My body yearned for the feeling of flesh against flesh. I moved slowly across the room, with catlike precision, to the heavy marble table that sat in front of my picture window. Dante watched my every move, and I made a conscious effort not to disappoint him. I sat my ass on the table, and the cool marble collided against my skin like fire and ice. As I reclined, I spread my legs before me and brazenly reached for my thong, pulling it to the side to offer Dante a glimpse of my fat punany.

"Miss me?" I asked.

Dante didn't say a word, but as the saying goes, actions speak louder than words, and I heard Dante's actions loud and clear. He pulled off his shirt, pushed off his shoes like a madman, and reached for his belt as he moved across the room and reached for a handful of my hair.

I moaned as he pulled my head back and kissed me passionately, leaving a trail of wet kisses from my lips to my chest. He pulled my bra back and circled my left nipple carefully with his tongue before engulfing the sweet morsel in his mouth. Dropping to his knees, he licked the very fingers that held my panties in position. I knew what was coming next, and my body became anxious with anticipation.

Dante teased my fingertips with wet kisses, pausing to inhale the warm scent of fresh, clean pussy on a platter. He took a moment to analyze my offerings before he parted my pussy lips with his thick, juicy lips. He began kissing, licking, and exploring all my womanly delights.

I purred as I arched my hips into his face and grabbed the back of his head. This was the picture I carried in my head, his handsome face as he licked me to satisfaction. Dante's mouth played tricks with my sweet little pussy, combining sultry sucks with gentle laps to my greedy clit. He sucked my pussy with expert precision, and it was more than I could stand.

I spread my legs more and put one hand behind me to support my shaky knees. The other hand moved from my panties to the nape of Dante's strong neck, and I pulled his head to me as I struggled to make his mouth and my pussy one. My release came hard and fast.

"Oh my God!" was all I could say. This man was a champ.

I was in the mood to bask in the glow of the light he had just shined on my night, but Dante was on a mission. He jumped to his feet and pulled out his dick like it was a lethal weapon.

"Damn," I said to myself at the sight of that pretty muthafuckin' head on his pipe. *Come do your damage.*

"You know what to do," was all he said.

Indeed I did. I rose up from the table and bent over, wrapping my thong around one steady ass cheek. I lifted one leg into position on the table and looked back to see Dante taking it all in.

"Fuck me, baby," was all he needed to hear.

While he tackled his jeans to dig for a condom, I pushed out my ass to be sure he knew I was ready and waiting.

"Hurry up, baby. I need you inside me."

Dante turned to face me and then slid the condom down the length of his fat dick. As he slipped inside of me, he said, "Here comes Daddy, baby. There you go. Take it. Take it."

And take it I did. He fucked me like there was no tomorrow, spreading my fat booty cheeks apart so he could get all the wetness I had to offer.

"Damn, you're wet!" Dante exclaimed. Indeed I was. I could feel my syrupy, sweet juices running down my leg. I was loving the long, hard strokes he was putting down.

The next thing I knew, all the hot pipe I had been getting was gone. One moment I had been filled up with Dante's vessel. The next minute I felt empty.

I turned around and was confused when I saw Dante drop to his knees once again. He spread my ass cheeks apart, and before I knew what he was about to do, he looked me in my eyes. And then it happened. He disappeared into my healthy abyss.

"Oh shit," I moaned. I hadn't ever taken a poll or anything, but in my book, ass licking is three or four fucks down the road, ain't it?

I could feel his warm tongue exploring, licking my asshole like he was searching for gold.

"You're such a nasty girl. I knew you would dig this shit," Dante said between licks.

"I do like it, Daddy, but I'd like the feel of your dick even better," was my reply. Once again, my boldness had stunned him.

There was a slight pause, and then the next thing I knew, he was rising to his feet. I could feel Dante's body heat surround me and his warm chest on my back.

"Good. Now be a big girl for Daddy, and take all this dick like the bad-ass bitch you are," he said, with more authority than he had ever used in his tone.

His long fingers began to massage my clit, and then the head of his fat dick began its descent to where the sun doesn't shine.

"Oh no, baby. Wait! Wait!" I hissed.

"Shhh, just relax, baby girl. I got you," he coaxed me. "Be a big girl for Daddy, baby, now."

I thought I was the baddest bitch a few seconds ago, when I was talking shit, but I wasn't ready for this. I thought I was. I mean, with the way his tongue and saliva had just loosened me up, I thought for sure I could take it. It was one of my fantasies, but now it was one of my fears. I hadn't expected the pressure to be so painful.

I thought about reneging, but the only thing I could think about was my wall calendar. I had to do it between now and the few weeks I had left. I figured I might as well get it over with now. But the first thing was first.

"Hold on a minute, Daddy." I held up my finger and retrieved the bottle of Tanqueray he had brought over with him. I needed some liquid courage.

"You need a glass?" he asked me, willing to help me out any way he could in order to speed this process up so that he wouldn't lose his hard-on.

I answered his question by putting the bottle to my lips and allowing the gin to burn my throat. I placed the cap back on the bottle and said, "Ahhh."

"You ready now, baby?"

I was not ready, yet somehow his soothing tone seemed to put me in a trance. I took one last deep breath and then braced myself. "I'm ready."

He picked back up where we had left off, massaging my clit with his fingers. His fingers were dripping with my juices and continued their gentle massage of wet pussy. A few seconds later, his head entered my ass, and I could feel my breath leave my body.

"I'm trying to be a big girl, baby, I am," I assured him.

"Yeah, that's Daddy's girl. Here you go, baby. Take all of it. Be a big girl, baby."

After I got over the initial shock of Dante's king-sized head, this anal stuff wasn't so bad. Combined with the generous attention his fingers were giving my pussy, I could get used to this.

My breath was coming in short, quick increments, and I continued to say to myself, "I'm Daddy's big girl. I'm being a big girl for Daddy," while Dante gently worked to maneuver within the tight confines of my virgin ass.

I decided to help him get where he needed to be in order to spare myself the embarrassment of failing short of my "big girl" responsibilities. Hell, the hard part was over, I thought. Getting the head in should have made way for the rest of his manhood. I began to slightly throw my ass back at him.

"Fuck your big girl, baby. Feed me all that fat pipe. Feed my ass, Big Daddy."

I could feel Dante's excitement at being given a permit to break loose, and that he did. He delved into my ass like it was his private playground. It only took a few hard strokes before the sounds of my coaxing and his release filled the air.

"Agghhh, that's it, baby. Here you go. That's it!" Dante exclaimed.

The room was completely still, and the house was silent. The moans that had filled the air only moments before were now replaced with the sounds of heavy breathing as we each collapsed on the couch, working to catch our breath.

I had completely lost myself in the act, not even considering that our loud moans could have awakened the kids.

At that very moment, despite everything that I felt had gone wrong in my life, everything was just right. Lying on the couch, in Dante's arms, felt like home, and I didn't want the feeling to end.

I closed my eyes so I could make a mental note of every detail. Dante's heartbeat rang loud and clear in my ear, and his body heat was the only blanket I needed.

I ran my fingers over his sinewy frame, making a mental image of every detail as my fingertips explored every perfect inch of his body. I inhaled the clean scent of him and then exhaled. I could feel his rapid breathing begin to calm and his hand resting on my hip.

"Where's your head at?" I asked him, curious to know if he had any thoughts on our sweat session.

"My head is still spinning," he replied, with a deep chuckle. "Seriously, though, you're cool as hell, Nina. Always have been. I always watched you doing your thing and thought, 'How can I be down?'"

I was puzzled. "How can you be down? What

kinda question is that to ask yourself? Were you scared?"

"Oh, hell no. Never that. Why you trying to play me?" he said on the offense. "To keep it all the way real, I always thought you were more into the pro black Professor Grif type of brothers."

I knew what he was referring to, but just in case I didn't, he made it clear.

"Look at your ex, Nina. The nigga is still rocking dashikis like it's straight up 1972!" We shared a mutual laugh over that one; he had jokes, which was cool. I liked a brotha with a sense of humor who wasn't always so damn serious all the time, like you know who. "Besides, you got married so young. You never let on that there was trouble in paradise until the end. I thought you two would be together forever, have eight kids and fourteen grandkids, fight the power, sell bean pies, and hell, I don't know."

Once again we shared a laugh. This dude knew more about me than I thought. He really must have been clocking and watching me on the downlow. Later I would find out that he also knew someone in my ex's family, who had briefed him on me and my situation with the rat bastard.

"All I know is I hear that nigga is sick about losing you right about now," Dante added.

And he was right. My ex had thrown a couple of hints to let me know he was available, but that was just because I had stopped chasing him, had stopped begging for my security blanket to come back, and had taken my divorce on the chin.

"And how is it that you know so much about how that man is feeling, Dante McGowan?" I asked.

"Because I'm with you right now, and as soon as I

walk out that door, I'll drive home, thinking about this ass, your smile, and your shit talking. And I know that nigga is still thinking about it, too." Dante kissed me on the forehead and then said, "You're one of a kind, Nina. You won't be single long, I can promise you that. I only wish that it could be me who takes you off the market."

Not sure where this conversation was heading, I challenged Dante to step up to the plate and stop beating around the bush.

"Dante, we never got to know each other as up close and personal as we have since we've been training together, but I consider myself a pretty good judge of character. And the one thing I never expected was for your ass to be no punk. *Now how about that,* I thought to myself.

I expected a man to be a man, and one thing a man did not do was make innuendos about his intentions. In other words, if Dante was trying to step to me, all the talk about "wishing" wasn't making an impression on me at all.

"Where the hell did you come up with that one?" Dante spat. "I ain't ever been called a punk, so how in the hell did you jump to that conclusion?"

This man had gotten beside himself and forced me to sit up and look him in the eye to be sure he comprehended the words I was about to speak.

"Dante, baby, why are you talking about what you 'wish' you could do? Hell, nigga, the way I see it, you got two choices: either shit or get off the damn pot. I can't even believe we're lying here ass naked as the day we were born, and you have the nerve to hint at a wish."

I rolled my neck and raised one eyebrow for added

emphasis. Dante let out a deep, ragged breath. Without breaking eye contact, he sat up on the couch and looked me dead in the eye for a while longer.

I raised my shoulders and extended both hands to my side. "You got something on your mind, playa?" I taunted.

"Yeah, as a matter fact I do," he began. "I just . . ." He dropped his head as if he was defeated. Dante raised his head and looked back in my eyes. All jokes aside, I could tell the mood had shifted, and he was dead serious. "Nina, I thought you knew. I mean, I just assumed that Monica told you."

I was perplexed. All I knew was something had just gone terribly wrong, and I was still trying to play catch-up. "Told me what, Dante? Speak on it. Cat gotcha tongue?" I hissed.

"Nina, I got a girl." He paused, but only for a second, and then continued. "And just recently I . . . I uh . . . I asked Bridget to marry me."

Okay, now for the first time in a long time, a bitch was speechless as he continued. "She's been in my corner for a long time, and we've had our ups and downs, but I ain't going nowhere, and neither is she. It took me awhile because she just changed up on me so much once she started going to college and got her degree. She just got so serious. No more fun and games. You know me. I'm like a big-ass kid. I handle my business, but after work, I'm ready to kick it."

Dante's words began to blend together, and he was beginning to sound like the annoying-ass adults in a Charlie Brown cartoon. *Is this shit for real?* is all I could think. *Somebody fucking pinch me, because I know I'm not hearing this shit.* Did this man, who just fucked the living daylights out of me and ate my pussy and my ass, just admit to being engaged?

"You're kidding me, right?" I said and grimaced.

He went to his pants and pulled out his wallet. He displayed to me what appeared to be an engagement picture; she was sporting her ring. The worst part of his confession was yet to come. I knew the ho he was engaged to.

Bridget was a mousy, funnily built chick with thick red hair and a sallow complexion. Her knees knocked so bad that you could hear her ass coming, which is probably why her man was between my knees. That bitch couldn't fuck with me on my worst day!

Bridget had grown up in my neighborhood. She had always just hung around. Her parents worked double time to send her to private school, so she had been there on the neighborhood scene but had not really been a part of the neighborhood crew.

She had even hung out with us in our adulthood. We had only allowed Bridget to hang with us because she was close with Destiny, Monica's godsister, another private school brat. The difference between the two of them was that Destiny was a wild-assed, try-anything-once preacher's kid and Bridget's scary ass was afraid of her own shadow.

Nevertheless, they had been bosom buddies since childhood, ever since Destiny had beaten the brakes off a school-yard bully who punked Bridget on a daily basis. Destiny had been the new girl in school and had been too hood for all the well-to-do girls in the small Christian private school, and Bridget had been the square peg with the high IQ that just didn't fit in anywhere.

Needless to say, they somehow managed to get

along famously. Every time we schemed to stay out late or meet up with the fellas, there was Bridget, with a never-ending list of all the cons, and as always, Destiny was there, too watching her girl's back, because she knew we couldn't wait to hem her bony ass up.

Now I will admit that Bridget was smart as hell. I can recall her tutoring my little brother when we were young, and I'll be damned if she didn't teach his little ass to read in no time flat. I had given up hope and had chalked my brother's illiteracy up to all the drug use Momma had subjected him to before she realized she was pregnant. Bridget got a full academic scholarship to Ohio University and went on to get her master's degree. Hell, if I'm not mistaken, the chick might have been in school so many years that she was be damn close to a PhD, but who's counting?

When I was off chasing Rahmel, and Destiny and I were busy making babies, Bridget and Monica had hung out on and off for awhile. I'd always summed that up to me not being available and Bridget's boring ass jumping every time Monica needed a partner in crime.

Dante's deep voice interrupted my trip down memory lane. "Nina, it's my turn to ask now. Where's your head at?"

I closed my eyes for an instant, and in that instant, I decided to push my conscience to the side. When I reopened my eyes, I decided that Dante's confession was his problem . . . not mine.

I leaned in close enough to feel my nipples caress Dante's bare chest. "My head is right here with you," I said as I planted a wet kiss on his thick lips. I slowly adjusted myself until I sat squarely on Dante's lap, straddling him, with one leg on the couch and the other barely touching the floor. "Now what do you want to do to me that you can't get away with at home?" Dante smiled, and I felt his excitement growing . . . literally.

Bridget could have him if she wanted him. I didn't want him. I just wanted his dick, which was exactly what I got.

I know I probably should have been mad at Dante for pulling that shit, but hell, what was there to be mad about? He had served his purpose. He had gotten me one step closer to fulfilling my every fantasy.

Chapter Nine

Moni In The Middle

I called Monica at exactly at 9:00 a.m. sharp, once I knew she was good and at work, to get the lowdown on why she'd kept Dante's status on the low.

"Well, good morning, sunshine," Monica greeted me, sarcastically enough for me to get the drift that she needed another cup of cappuccino or two.

"Hey, girl. What's going on?" I asked, ignoring the attitude in her voice.

"What's wrong?" Monica went straight for the meat of the matter. Being my girl for upteen years, she could tell I had something to say.

So the same way she decided to get straight to the point of things, so did I. "Were you planning on telling me anytime soon that Dante and Bridget had gotten engaged?" I asked.

I heard Monica smack her lips like she had an attitude, but I didn't give a damn. I light weight had one of my own.

"Nina, since when does Bridget's business concern you? I mean, Dante ain't nothing but a drinking buddy and workout partner, right?"

I hated to play this game with my girl. She knew I wanted details, but she was determined to get her own questions answered first. So I sat back while she went about her not-so-gentle method of prodding me for information.

"Is there something Dante has been working on with you outside the gym, Nina?" she asked. "The word on the streets is that his car has been spotted in your driveway. What's up with that?"

Now I got an instant attitude. "Monica, I asked you a simple question. Now how are you going to turn my question into one of your own?"

Monica wanted information, and nothing I said was going to get her off track.

"Look, Nina, you know Dante and Bridget have been dating on and off for the past three, almost four years now. He asked her to marry him around New Year's, but hell, I figured it wasn't worth mentioning since they've been together forever, that is, unless you done started spending some time with him and caught feelings. I hope that's not the case."

If I had known I was going to meet up with "I got up on the wrong side of the bed" Monica, I would have held my peace until lunchtime.

"Umm, hello. Did I dial the right extension?" I asked her, tapping the phone for effect. "I was trying to reach my best friend, Monica Lafayette. I must have misdialed. Could you patch me through to her?" I was being sarcastic as hell, but why not?

Monica laughed under her breath, the way she always did when she was at work, trying to keep her personal conversation on the low. "I'm serious, Nina. You got some explaining to do," Monica continued. "You been fucking that boy outside of our little . . . you know . . . haven't you?"

I lied. "Naw." But she was my BFF, so I had to tell the truth. "Just once or twice."

"Nina, you promised, and so did Dante, not to keep—"

I cut her off mid-sentence. "Come on now, Moni. We are all adults. I dig him, and we enjoy each other, so that's that." It would have been too much like right for Monica to let it go at that.

"Oh, hell no! You got me bent. That is not that! Let me be the first to admit, Dante is fine, but he is completely off-limits. We can't be having relations with someone who is engaged to someone in our circle. I felt bad enough about what went down between all of us, but I considered it water under the bridge. I chalked it up to some drunk shit that we could all look at each other and chuckle about, but now you two are taking this to a whole notha level."

I couldn't believe the whole thing, how Monica was taking shit to heart. "Since when was Bridget in *our* circle?" I asked Monica. "From what I recall, we spend most of our time trying to avoid Bridget's awkward ass. Now she is part of our crew? Did I miss something?"

Monica changed the tone of her voice from a high-pitched whisper to that of an overly patronizing mother. "Now, Nina, that was when we were kids. You been out of the way for a while, baby." Monica dragged the word *baby* off her lips like she was comforting a damn two-year-old. "Bridget and I been hanging out for awhile now. You know that."

"When's the last time you called Bridget since Rahmel and I split up, Monica?"

"That's not the point. The point is we are cool, and since she's my girl, it's putting me in an uncomfortable position. Can you understand that?"

Monica had a point, but I wasn't bending. "If she's your girl, why the big secret about the engagement? Why not spread the joy?"

Monica's carrying on about Bridget was making me sick. She only gave a damn about Bridget because all her road dogs were either hemmed up or taking care of kids.

"Well, you got me on that one," Monica agreed. "I'll be the first to admit that when Dante started training you, I was like, 'Okay. Let's see what happens here,' but then he asked Bridget to marry him and that sent me for a loop. It seemed like you had a little crush, so I just let it happen. But now it's getting hectic, and I just want it to stop."

Monica wasn't through, and she continued. "Bridget was always carrying on like his dick was made of gold and shit, and I wanted to see if it was true. But you got what you wanted. You know he is spoken for. Now let what happened stay in the past before you catch feelings. Dante is not leaving Bridget, trust me. I've seen him out and about on more than one occasion when they were on the outs, with a dime piece on his arm, but he still ends up with Bridget. She is not going anywhere, Nina. You've had your fun. Now it's time to leave the man alone. He is marrying Bridget."

Monica's motherly preaching was starting to piss me off. So I had to retaliate. "In other words it was cool for me to fuck him as long as you were down were controlling the situation, is that what I'm hearing? Monica, since when do you give a fuck about fucking somebody's somebody? And whether or not it was a big deal to you, we always tell each other everything. So why'd you hold out on this tidbit of information?"

"Why did I hold out? Is that the pot calling the kettle black or what? Nina, have you stopped to realize that you failed to mention during any of our umpteen chats that you screwed Dante at your house?"

No use denying it. I was busted. "Shit, Monica, I didn't mean to keep it on the low. Really. It was that bullshit promise you made us swear to that kept me from spilling the beans." I felt bad. Besides not telling her about my almost sexual encounter with Monte, this was only the second time I had kept a secret this major from my ace. The first time was when I started digging Rahmel. Monica thought that he was such a hot mess that I couldn't possibly be digging him. When I realized I did, it took me months to own up to it.

"Listen, Nina, Bridget done gave that brother big ups about having some top-notch skills in the bedroom. Hell, she acts like his dick is made of gold. Obviously, it is, because you ain't trying to give it up. Look, I just don't want this to disrupt our circle, you know?"

"I'm just doing me right now, Moni, and the last thing I plan on doing is getting sloppy with this, having you in the middle of it. But for right now, we enjoy each other. Bridget is not even a topic of discussion when we're together. We're digging each other right now."

Monica snorted like she was appalled. "What?

You're digging each other? Trust me, Nina, he ain't going to mess up that gravy train with a PhD. Don't get caught up in the hype. Bridget's pursuit of the American dream has obviously given Dante more rope than he can handle. So don't get it twisted, Nina. He ain't leaving her. Let it go."

I could tell Monica was dead serious, but so was I. If she couldn't understand where I was coming from, this would just have to be one of those times when we agreed to disagree.

"Monica, I hear you, and as my girl, I respect you for trying to point me in the right direction. With that said, right now I just wanna do what I wanna do, and that just might happen to be Dante."

"Okay, so be it, but I can already see the writing on the wall, and you're digging that man more than you're willing to admit. Trust me when I say women ain't built like men. After a while, you're gonna start catching some feelings. But I have to remember that you're new to this. So let me break it down further. Fucking and being in a relationship are two entirely different things. You can't allow yourself to lose sight of that, and I think maybe you have. I been out here living this single life long enough to know, I need you to trust me on this one."

Ooohh boy, I thought to myself. This conversation was going nowhere fast. "Moni, I got this. *Trust me.*"

"Nina, how are you going to feel after they get married and we all hook up? You can't be mad at Bridget because you crept with her man, you know?"

"I'm a big girl, Monica. I appreciate all the advice you've given me up until now, but I'm going to follow my own intuition on this one, okay?"

"All right, Nina, but I can't be a part of this. Bridget and me are cool, so keep the details to yourself."

Monica was trying to take a stand, but it wouldn't last long with me . . . It never did. So I agreed, for now, just to keep the peace. "Point taken. Have a good day, sunshine!" The tone of my voice was syrupy sweet, even though I was being a smart-ass.

"Bye, bitch," was Monica's reply.

I knew it was the end of our conversation, but the beginning of some bullshit.

Chapter Ten

Who's That Girl?

It was only the second week in February, one of the coldest months of the year, and yet things were starting to heat up in my life. My day had been awful, gloomy, cold, and full of demands. I could remember it all too well: it seemed as if every project I started had to be completed yesterday. The only light at the end of the tunnel was the fact that it was Thursday, and tomorrow, at 5:00 p.m., I could temporarily escape from the demands of my job. My last phone call put a twinkle in my eye and a smile on my face.

"Yes!" I had just landed the advertising campaign for a major corporation, and it made all the drama of the day melt away. I picked up the phone to call Monte and brag to him. "Boy, you had better take advantage of my skills before I start to demand a price you can't afford," I told him in reference to my doing some advertising work for his business.

Monte chuckled. "As long as I can still take advantage of your body from time to time, I don't have any problems letting you be the breadwinner."

I replied huskily, "Is that an invitation?"

"Oh, fo' sho'!" Monte let the thug out of the box, and I could feel my insides warming.

Lord, I don't know what it is about a man with a hint of thug—an urban cowboy. I think it must be the feminine need for a lover and protector, or the rebellion of having a "bad boy."

"What time you leaving the plantation?" Monte asked me. "I got a surprise for you."

My mind was racing too fast to contemplate exactly what it could be. All I knew was that I could feel the tiny hairs on my neck start to rise. My insides got wet, and my mind wandered a million miles from my small office, into an erotic abyss.

I spread my legs and thanked God for thigh-highs, because I needed to cool off before my mind got ahead of me.

"I'm wrapping things up as we speak," I told him. "Give me twenty minutes or so to finalize a few things, and I'll see you later on."

Monte replied, "Put some sexy shit on for me, baby. You know it's been a while."

Monte and I had very hectic lives. Between me juggling time with the kids and work, and his business slash hustle, we managed to see each other in the between times.

"All right, babe. See you later," I said, trying to end the conversation.

"Nah, you gon' *feel* me later."

Ah. There was that thug again. A sistah could hardly wait.

After leaving work, I made my thirty-minute drive

home. Once there, I ran around my home, preparing myself like I was going to have sex for the first time. I showered and shaved, then proceeded to soak in a hot bubble bath and fantasize to get myself in a sexual zone.

I turned on R. Kelly's *TP-2.com,* lit candles, and relaxed on my lounger as I oiled my body and smiled with anticipation. I lay back on my bed and allowed myself to be swept away by the music. While lying there, I explored my body as if it were new to me. Monte was by no means my dream man, but from the limo to the romantic dinners, his whimsical antics definitely kept me on my toes.

As the hour came near, I got up and went to my armoire to pull out a sexy piece of lingerie. Gold seemed only fitting for the mood I was in. I put on a gold two-piece set, low cut on top to accentuate my breasts and high cut on the bottom to show off my thick thighs and provide a peekaboo glimpse of my well-rounded ass.

I looked at myself in the mirror. My brown eyes were heavy with lust, and my lips were ripe and inviting. "Damn, you're a sexy bitch," I said to myself.

I could already feel Monte's lips on my body and his tongue . . .

My thoughts were interrupted by the sound of my doorbell. I took my time as I went casually down the corridor to my front door, not wanting to appear too eager.

I smiled at the sight of Monte leaning against my screen door, on one arm, a rose in his mouth and his dick in his hand. We both laughed at the sight of each other, me in my gold lingerie and him in a faded denim jeans outfit, with a silk gold T-shirt underneath.

"Get off my wavelength!" I said and laughed, letting him into the house.

"Damn, baby, that just lets you know that tonight was meant to be! My baby was feeling her daddy, huh?"

I laughed as he cupped my ass in his hands and grabbed me around my waist. "I got a surprise for your, baby," Monte said smoothly.

"I like surprises. Is it a big one?" I asked.

"Oh yeah. Look outside," Monte instructed.

The first thing I was thinking was, Damn, this nigga done bought a bitch a car? I didn't know he was ballin' out of control like that.

I went to the window, thinking I would find . . . well, hell, I don't know just what exactly I thought I was going to find or what I was hoping for, but I know it was anything but what I got.

I saw Monte's car in my driveway, with the lights on and a stunning young woman looking boldly back at me. It goes without saying that my mug was completely twisted.

"Who the hell is that?" I said. I immediately put the brakes on, and the mood stopped, as if somebody had made the record scratch in the middle of a slow jam.

"Come on, baby," Monte called, coaxing me as he walked over and joined me at the window. "We talked about this, remember? I thought you'd be happy."

I was still confused as to why this fool thought I would be excited about him toting another bitch around in his ride. He gave me further clarification.

"I got us a bad bitch to share. I talked to Patrice, and she was down with it," he explained. "You remember Patrice. You met her the night we painted the town at the Chrome."

After Monte and I had taken on a sexual relationship, we had discussed the pros and cons of a threesome.

"The concept is hot, until somebody gets their feelings hurt," I had told him. "I mean, think about it, Mo. When it's three of you in the bed, somebody is gonna get left out at some point in time."

Monte had countered, "Nah, baby. It's all about positioning and picking the right freak for the j-o-b. Now if this was to go down, who would you choose?"

I had imagined that this was a question most couples discussed among themselves. And at some point, when the question was answered, it turned into a heated argument, with one person questioning why their mate would want to have sex with their best friend. Nonetheless, I never replied to Monte's original query, not verbally, anyway, but in my head I'd said Nikki. I'd listened to her sensual stories for so long that I craved to be a part of one.

Nonetheless, Monte presented me with an unexpected gift on this night, in the form of Patrice.

I vaguely recalled the night I met Patrice, because Monte and I had partied and club hopped all night long. While I tried to jog my memory, Monte went to the door, waved his hand, and put up his index finger, signaling to Patrice to hold up a second. She smiled and acknowledged him. She spotted me assessing the situation through the window and shot me a friendly smile and wave. That's when my memory was jogged.

I recognized Patrice and clearly remembered meeting

her. She was all the way live. The night at the club, I barely got introduced to her before she grabbed my hand and led me to the opposite side of the club, where they were hosting the review. She yelled in my ear about the brother she had been tipping all night, with the "anaconda" in his pants. That night I barely got a good glimpse of her in the dim club lights, and I was wearing beer goggles no less.

From what I recalled, she was pretty well put together, but I was not in the mood to have her in my mix tonight.

"Uh-uh Mo. Pump the brakes, pimp," I said to Monte. "This was not what I planned when we discussed this shit. I had no intention of you throwing some foreign pussy in my bedroom, with no consultation!"

Monte made his best attempt to seduce me with his mack vibe. "Come on, baby girl. Me and you sat down together, and we were on the same page with trying some new shit. We explored the details and worked out the kinks. Now all we gotta do is seal the deal. If it gets down to the get down and you ain't feeling it, then call it off, but Patrice is cool. She just got off of a long-term relationship herself, and she's just looking for some action. You know, to explore new things. To keep it on the real, babe, we just scored us a freak to use up a little bit, ya feel me?"

I was not yet convinced, and to make matters worse, one of my best girls, Tee, burst in the front door and exclaimed, "Giiirrll, these two dates of mine is getting kinda hectic!"

It was official. I thought to myself. My night was ruined. *This cannot be happening to me,* I said to myself as I lowered my head into my hands and prayed for it to all be over.

Tee had been talking ninety miles per hour, but finally, she shut up long enough to step back and assess the situation: R. Kelly playing on the stereo; me in lingerie, with my hands on my hips; and Monte with this sheepish ass look on his face. Although Tee was fully aware of my explorations in sexuality, I had not prepared to reveal the present situation.

Tee was clearly excited about juggling two dates, because she had always been the exclusive girlfriend or mistress of some well-paid something or other. I put on a half-baked smile in a meager attempt to share in Tee's excitement. All the while I pondered my predicament. Tee finally stepped up to the plate and said, "Look, I don't know what I interrupted, but let me freshen up and I'm out. Your house just happened to be in the middle of my two destinations."

I followed Tee to the bathroom as a temporary excuse to wrap my mind around this turn of events. "Damn," Tee proceeded to say, "there used to be a time when I could drop my black ass by anytime I pleased, without a second thought of stepping on anybody's toes. I guess times have changed."

Tee proceeded to talk fourteen-karat gold shit in between mouthwash and lip gloss applications. Tee rushed out of the bathroom as quickly as she had gone in, pausing only long enough to pop a peppermint Altoid in her mouth. She looked me and Monte up and down and further assessed the situation.

"Y'all look so cute," she complimented. "Y'all got awfully coordinated just to screw, don't y'all think?" Before we could respond, she blurted out, "I know my black ass is interrupting the flow around this piece. Now shit, I'm out! I gotta meet my second date downtown."

She proceeded to the door and was out as quickly as she had come in, leaving me right in the middle of this bullshit with Monte.

Monte put one strong arm around my waist and led me over to the couch. He had the audacity to hand me a drink, which he must have thrown together during Tee's hasty visit.

"I took Patrice upstairs, to the bedroom, while you and Tee were in the back," he said calmly.

The look on my face after he said that spoke volumes, and he knew it.

"Come on now, baby," he said. "This was our plan. Do this for Daddy."

To be perfectly real about the situation, I was a little pissed, but I was turned on at the same time, if you know what I mean. Like I said before, I'm a control freak. I like to say when, but more importantly, I like to say who. And on top of that, how dare this bastard invite this woman into my house!

"Look, Monte, just keeping it real, I am not cool with how you trying to make this go down. How the fuck are you just going to bring her over my house without talking to me first?" As I continued to bitch, Monte worked his way down my body with his hands in an attempt to tone down my anger. He lifted my leg over one shoulder and carefully, slowly licked the sensitive outer lips of my pussy. As he continued to unwrap them and explore with his tongue, I looked down at him to find his eyes focused on my face. This punk was trying his best to gauge my feelings.

He continued to lick and probe my insides with his tongue until he rekindled my fire. A small, helpless moan came from my parted lips as I sat back to enjoy his exploration. Now this was what tonight was supposed to be about—me only.

Monte lifted me in his strong arms and carried me down the hallway, kissing me as if he was trying not to break the spell. I tasted his kiss and was reminded of the peppermint treat I had rubbed on myself earlier to give him a minty surprise.

"What you got down there?" he asked, looking all of twelve years old.

"Did you enjoy that?" I asked.

"Oh yeah, pussies need that," he replied, making me laugh softly to myself.

He laid me on the bed in my candlelit room and stared into my eyes. I could tell he was trying to read me, and I tried to make my expression as blank as possible.

"Look, babe," he said. "I got more rubbers than the clinic, and I grabbed some dental dams, too. I want you all right with this. You my baby, and I was just trying to turn you out in my own way. My bad if I overstepped my boundaries. I was trying to outfreak your nasty ass."

I won't lie. His explanation worked on me a little bit. I had put it out there that I was trying to get my freak on. I had shared all of my thoughts and inhibitions with him. Monte just forgot the cardinal rule: I say when and how and who.

I decided to let it slide for right now and took his advice about using that freak and having some fun in the process.

"Are you down?" he asked, with a solemn look on his face.

I thought for a second before saying, "Yeah, Mo,

I'm down. But don't expect too much on my part. I barely know that girl."

Just as quickly as I agreed to the threesome, Monte was on his feet to fetch Patrice from the back bedroom. As Monte disappeared down the hall and left me with my thoughts for a moment, I took a long swig of my drink. At that moment, I wasn't feeling so confident. If the other girl had been Monica, it would have been a piece of cake. I had no problems exploring with her, and we knew each other's boundaries, not that either of us necessarily had any. *Mental note to self,* I thought as I took another long drink. *New pussy must be spelled out as one of my boundaries going forward.*

Now don't get it twisted. My husband and I experimented with a baby ménage à trois during our college days. It was a good time in our marriage. We did it with a very close friend of ours. The three of us discussed it in depth before the event took place, and we were all very comfortable with each other, so that allowed us to fully enjoy the experience. As long as Monte had this plethora of condoms close by at all times, I was cool with that. One thing was for sure, though: there was going to be no double-dipping.

My thoughts were invaded as Monte, with Patrice in tow, came into the room. Patrice was looking bashful, and Monte appeared much too gung ho about the whole thing.

"Where is that stuff you had on your—," Monte began, but I put my hand in the air to cut him off. I knew where he was going with that statement.

"It's in my dresser, dear," I replied.

As Monte scrambled around, searching through my own personal treasure chest, I allowed myself to observe Patrice. She was petite, with a small frame, shapely hips, and well-rounded ass. She was Monte's type for sure. Hell, the more I looked, the more I realized she could be my type, too.

Patrice had pretty hazel eyes and wavy black hair, which she pulled back into a sleek ponytail. She appeared to have a natural rosy glow on her cheeks and lips. She was a mulatto beauty, if in fact she was mixed. I was not exactly sure.

Patrice refused to make eye contact with me, letting me know she was just as unsure of the situation as I was. In the meantime, Monte finally struck gold and turned, with a wide grin on his handsome face. He had a small round jar of cream in his hand that the woman was supposed to apply to her vagina before sex. It not only produced a tingling sensation on the clit, but it also rewarded the woman's partner with a tasty treat that was similar to chocolate with a hint of mint.

Monte took Patrice by her shoulders and led her to my bed and sat her on the edge, next to me. He took the drink, which he had obviously made her, from her hand and placed it on the nightstand. Monte then went about removing her clothes slowly, as if he was trying not to disturb the groove.

Patrice lay on my bed in a T-shirt and socks, which Monte had neglected to remove. Patrice's creamy complexion glistened in the glow of my candlelit room. What Mo did next let me know that this brother must have put some serious thought into this night.

Monte moved with ease and precision, gently laying me back on the bed and removing my gold undies. His hands carefully arranged our legs across one another, so we both had our legs spread and over-lapping in the middle. Monte applied the cream to our bodies lavishly, and Patrice squeaked, her first show of emotion.

"Ooh! It's making my pussy tingle. Damn, it's hot!" she said.

I laughed at her excitement, then proceeded to laugh harder at Monte's cool reply to her, which was a little like déjà vu. "Yeah, pussies need that."

With that said, Monte winked his eye at me, bent down, got on his knees, and then licked Patrice's pussy as if he had found an oasis in the midst of the Sahara Desert.

"Ummm," cried Patrice. She let out a hoarse moan. She then grabbed his head and stroked it slowly.

"I'll be right back," Monte told Patrice sweetly. He then made his way to my perfectly edged pussy and gave me the same delightful treat.

I could feel Patrice's legs jump in anticipation of having him back at her throne, so my instincts told me to reach my hand in between her legs and caress her pussy to temporarily soothe her anticipation.

Monte continued this torment between the two of us, volleying back and forth like a tennis ball, leaving us both wanting when he moved on to please the other. Like a master magician, he moved us into phase two of his tricks.

He centered us in the middle of the bed, legs wide and asses cheek to cheek. He proceeded once again to lick, this time faster and with a direct trail from one eager pussy to the other.

Damn! This shit was sweet torture. We both moaned and pulled at his head so he would come back and finish us off. Phase three was even sweeter still.

Monte laid Patrice across my body. Both our shirts had been removed. At what point that happened, I actually can't recall. Patrice's warm body was pressed against mine. Her pale breasts pressed against my light golden globes, and both our lips, soft and wet, met and puckered in warm kisses.

Monte then began his assault again, licking hungrily from her to me. His tongue was sheer fire on our bodies. Patrice kissed me passionately, and I returned the gesture. Her hips began to move against mine, sending shock waves through my clitoris. Monte's objective was clearly to break the ice between her and me, and at this point, it was completely melted and dripping.

The next thing I knew, I saw Patrice's eyes fly open wide, and she let out a moan from deep within. "Aaagh, yes!" she screamed.

Monte had finally let go of his restraints on himself and was fucking Patrice wildly from behind. Her hips continued to move against mine, matching his rhythm. The look on her face was sheer bliss as she received him, and I found myself watching her with envy. My moment of jealousy was short-lived, though. Monte broke his stride long enough to reload his condom, drop down a notch, and deliver the same blow to my hungry kitten. Patrice kissed my lips and pressed her hips against mine. No words can describe the wave of passion I was riding. It was drowning me, literally clouding my senses, yet too unbelievable to resist.

Monte seemed to be full of surprises that evening. Before I could become accustomed to the glorious sensations running through my body, I was placed in another position, which was as remarkable as the first. Monte, with the gentle skill of a master trainer, moved our bodies carefully into an upright position. Patrice and I were both seated on top of Monte's muscular physique, his dick still deep inside of me.

Patrice scrambled around and seated herself prettily on top of Monte's face. In turn, I spun around on his dick so I could ride him backwards and casually massage his balls. The moans that came from both Patrice and me filled the air.

I looked at my body in the mirrors opposite my bed, and I was forced to appreciate the beauty of sex. Patrice and I were both on top of Monte, with our backs leaning against one another for support. While she allowed her hips to slowly circle his tongue, I wanted to enjoy the full length of him, so I rode him like there was no tomorrow. At some point, our arms became intertwined, and our bodies moved to the same frenzied salsa. As I gazed at our bodies in the mirror, I realized that this was not just sex. It was in fact art.

Patrice and I switched positions. However, it didn't take long before I craved the taste of Monte's balls in my mouth, so I gave up my seat on Monte's dick and crawled behind Patrice. Leaning her body forward, I spread Monte's legs wide, then commenced licking and sucking his sack.

"Damn, baby girl. You making it hard for a brother to maintain!" Monte exclaimed.

I continued the task at hand, then moved on to plant gentle kisses down the length of Patrice's spine. We continued this dance of moving from one glorious position to another. I felt as if I was wrapped in a cocoon of passion, being carried away on a wave of lust. What happened next left a permanent imprint on my body and soul.

The tingle I felt down my spine was matched by the throbbing between my legs. Patrice crawled between my legs and planted her pink lips on my pussy.

"Oh yeah," I said as I exhaled and arched my back to meet her tongue. Trust me when I say this, and I swear it to be true: nobody eats pussy like pussy.

Monte swiftly took advantage of Patrice's ass in the air and took her from behind. The image of those two only served to increase my desire. Monte must have envied Patrice and the way she greedily licked my sweet spot, like a bear who had stolen a pot of warm honey. I screamed at the sensation as he bent over her ass and joined her between my legs.

They both lapped at my pussy like two puppies drinking from the same bowl. Oh my goodness, it was unbearable. I came hard and fast before I even realized that an orgasm was upon me. I only allowed myself a moment to recoup before I announced that I wanted, no needed, to feel Monte inside of me.

I pushed him back on the bed, paused to reload the condom, and rode him hard and fast. Patrice began to kiss his lips and tease his mouth with her rosy nipples. Watching them only made my climax sweeter. I laid my head on Patrice's back, placed two fingers inside her pussy, and nearly cried as heaven and earth collided in one fleeting moment.

Monte looked fairly drained from the whole affair. Meanwhile Patrice and I lay together, exploring each other gently, engaging in the after-sex shit that few men are hip about.

"You opened me up to something that I ain't know was there," Patrice said boldly to me. At the time I didn't know that this experience would be like a gateway drug for more encounters with my own kind.

Unlike the encounter I had had when I was younger, this torrid threesome had opened me up to a few things myself. I wondered what it would be like to have a bitch all to myself. While I was thinking about this, I made a mental note to myself. *Get the coldest bitch you can find, and turn her ass out!*

I could scarcely recall the kiss Monte planted on my forehead or the two of them saying their good-byes. It was the crack of dawn, and my body was limp from the night before. I woke up to find Patrice's number next to me, on the nightstand. *All right, little momma. I like that in you,* I thought to myself.

My bedroom was a mess. It looked as if the damn Jolly Green Giant had lifted the roof off my house and showered it with condoms. There were all kinds: scented, flavored, glow in the dark, you name it. I laughed to myself every time I happened upon one.

I picked up the phone and left a message for Monte. "All right, old man, you represented. You earned an *S* on your chest last night, Superman. Call me when you wake up, baby. I'm sure you'll be out of it for awhile."

I hung up the phone and jerked at the thoughts of my experience. Four hands roaming about the body were better than two. So what could possibly beat six hands? The ultimate in sexual fulfillment and erotic adult fun is the ménage à trois. A hand on your titty, a tongue in your ass, and a dick in your pussy. Mmmm. I can literally taste it.

The sense of anticipation I felt was akin to that of a small child smelling chocolate chip cookies baking in the oven, inhaling the sweet aroma, not being able to wait to get them in your hands and taste the heavenly treat.

The softness of a woman combined with the power and strength of a man is fire and ice, and the orgasm it brings opens the clouds, rains on my body, and thunders through my entire being.

I picked up the phone and then proceeded to leave a message of a different sort for Patrice, about a private meeting at a later date. I was sure Mo would be pissed if he found out, but hell he was the one who opened up Pandora's box.

Chapter Eleven

The Watcher

A few degrees cooler than having sex is watching it up close and personal. Seeing the expressions, muscles moving, and hearing the moans in three dimensions are indescribable feelings.

If I was ever going to have a sexual tag team partner, it would be one of my best girls, Nikki. She is crazy, sexy, cool. If I could grow a dick for a day, she'd be the first woman on my list to get freaky with.

To look in her eyes was to see that there was something so deep going on inside of her that you had to be on her level to really feel it. If you weren't fortunate enough to be on her level, you'd still know it was there. You might even want to taste it, but either you got it or you didn't.

I'd witnessed many a brother walk away from Nikki, perplexed, utterly rejected, but somehow still captivated by her charm. If a brother couldn't get on her level, he would never know what treasures she had buried beneath her sweet, "innocent" exterior.

My girl Nikki had a few years on me, which means she took her time and had learned to be very subtle, yet sensual, an art that I could confess to being very good at, but I was still perfecting it. Whereas it might take her months to work on her man, preparing him for all she had to offer, grooming him until he was ready to erupt, I was still young and willing.

Nikki and I spent hours on the phone, and over lunch, we discussed our sexual exploits. Whether it was the crank caller that happened upon Nikki in the middle of the night and got more than he expected from a lewd remark, or hot sex in the back of a limo, we told all and promised each other that one day, when one of us came upon the right brother, he was going to get it good from both of us.

Our conversations were not just steamy girl talk, but she did offer me a glance at her bedroom prowess, a glimpse that left me positive she was what fantasies were made of.

It was about eight o'clock Sunday evening. I had partied all weekend with Mo, and I was preparing my mind for another work week. I called Nikki to tell her about the fun I had had the night before and all the liquor I had left at my house from the weekend trip with Monte. We had driven down to Cleveland to watch Iverson and LeBron go head to head. We had a damn good time, and if I say so myself, seeing Iverson in full effect made me want to drop my façade and act like a damn groupie.

"Damn!" Nikki said. "It sounds like your house is where I need to be. I could use a drink to get my mind right."

Although my body was tired, I had never been one to turn down a friend in need.

"Come on over, chick. You know I got you."

As I thought about it, I realized this was the perfect chance for her to hook up with Monte's younger brother, Marcus. Marcus had seen Nikki work the room at the club one night. He had tried to holler, but she'd been in her element and had shot him down quick. He wanted a second chance at the title, and I had promised him some face time, but nothing more. This was his chance.

Knowing how particular my girl was, I picked up the phone to see if she was down.

"Sounds like a plan," was her simple reply.

I called Monte and gave him the scenario: a Sunday nightcap with his brother and Nikki. He said that he was game, and that he would call his brother and see if he could swing through.

I jumped in the shower to get rejuvenated, dipped into a Vicki's secret capri set, and lit some scented candles to get the energy flowing. While I waited for my company to shoot through, I wrote up my weekly to do list, called Miles and Ariel to give them some Mommy love before they went to bed, and made myself a stiff drink.

A long pour of Tanqueray, a quick shot of grapefruit, and a bitch smack of cranberry were all I needed to get in the zone. I mixed my concoction up good and gave myself a mental pat on the back. If my momma didn't teach me a damn thing, she knew how she wanted her drink and raised me up to be a good little barmaid.

Relaxing on my bed, with my drink in my hand, I picked up the remote and flipped through the channels. The Spice Channel caught my attention, so I decided to sit back and sip my drink while I enjoyed viewing an old English gentleman with a parliamentary wig and powdered face, swagging a damsel in distress, complete with corset and petticoats.

Just as my hand slid into my panties, I was brought back to reality by three quick knocks on the door. Drink in hand, I made my way to the door. Looking out the peephole, I laid eyes on my girl Nikki. I opened the door and let her in.

"Hey, Mama," I said, giving her a quick hug.

"Trying to be like you when I grow up," Nikki said, eying my drink.

"I got you, baby." I made my way to the kitchen so Nikki could get her mind right. An expert like me, she went about my kitchen like it was her own, mixing the ingredients for a stiff, cold drink.

Now, let's talk about sexy. Nikki, in laymen's terms, was drop-dead gorgeous. Her light pecan complexion was blemish free, and she had an easy, seductive smile. Nikki's petite frame was accentuated by wide hips, which glided around my kitchen like they were dancing to their own melody. Her deep-set eyes were all knowing. In other words, she didn't miss shit.

Her heart-shaped face was framed by long jet-black hair, and she could easily be described as one of those chicks that looks like she's got Indian in her family. Nikki was never one to carry on about her natural good looks; the only thing I ever heard Nikki brag about was the "pretty set of titties" she had inherited from her momma.

This bitch had a set of titties on her that women were paying for as we speak.

During a trip with the rest of crew to visit the Taste of Chicago, we had all been amazed by the moisturizing routine she gave them pretty mothafuckers every night.

"Who the fuck she think she is?" my girl Jonnie had said with hate in her eyes.

"Shit," Monica had replied casually. "I ain't even gon' front. Y'all my girls, but to keep it all the way real, I wanted to rub that lotion on them titties my damn self!"

We all shared a good laugh at that one. Bottom line. . . . The girl is bad.

Sipping on her drink to ensure it met her expectations, Nikki joined me at the kitchen table. "So, did the birthday girl enjoy her weekend with her man?" she asked, with a sly grin on her pretty face.

"Oh yeah, most definitely," I replied. "I thoroughly enjoyed myself. Girl, I haven't kicked it like that since I turned sweet sixteen."

Now that was the truth. My momma and I might have had our ups and downs, but she came through for her firstborn baby on that birthday.

"That's real good. You deserved it, girl," Nikki replied.

My weekend with Monte actually had been the bomb. Despite the brother's pipe being real average, he was such a fucking gentleman. I loved the fact that he was a thugged-out Casanova in his own right.

I loved the man's spontaneity; that was no lie. Now if he could only bring that same element into the bedroom, he might keep his footing.

"That's your nigga," Nikki remarked. "I like him taking care of you. You need that shit right now, feel me?"

My girl Nikki was all about a brother catering to her, so in her book, Monte was all right.

"I can't tell a lie, Nick. I dig that about Mo. He is definitely on point. But if it wasn't for his head game, I wouldn't be cummin' at all."

Nikki almost spit out her drink. "Girl, you're lying. All that good shit and he can't fuck?"

I shook my head. "Sad, but true," was my only reply.

Monte's ears must have been on fire, because my cell phone lit up, and I looked down to see "Mo Daddy" on my caller ID.

"Hey, baby. What's going on?" I asked.

"Same shit, different toilet, baby doll," Mo replied. "Look, babe, I'm knee-deep in some bullshit over here, but I'm gon' try my best to shoot through. But my bro is thirsty to get with Nikki, so he's going to shoot through for a minute, if you don't mind."

I was more than cool with that. The less I had to entertain, the better. "That's cool, Big Poppa," I replied. "What about you? You all right?"

Monte was cool as usual. "Yeah, baby doll, cooler than a fan. I'm just handling my business."

I knew all too well what "handling my business" entailed, and that let me know that this fling would end as soon as the thrill was gone.

"All right. Poppa. Be safe."

"Sure thing, baby doll. Good night," Mo replied, and then we ended our call.

I took a second to marinate on the fact that Mo had ended the conversation with a "good night" rather than "I'll see you later," which, in my book, meant his "business" was going to take him all night.

I realize that I was being paranoid for no reason because I was doing my own thing. I decided not to be concerned with Montes' whereabouts this evening, not to mention he was laying pipe like his mama never gave him a Lego set. But wait one good goddamn minute. I was a territorial bitch by nature, so as usual, I made a mental note to self to see how often "business" took precedence over his spending time with me.

"Mo can't make it. Business. But Marcus is on his way," I told Nikki. Like clockwork, Marcus knocked on the door. I handed Nikki my glass as I made my way to the door. "Make me one of your world-class drinks while I let your boy toy in," I said.

I opened the door to let Marcus in, all the while admiring the view. *Um um um, Little Brother Almighty!* I thought to myself, reflecting on the fine-ass frat boys in *School Daze.* Little brother was definitely well packaged. Whereas big bro was hip-hop slash R & B, little brother was all about the hip-hop.

His light brown skin was lightly beaded with freckles, which gave him a boyish look despite his roughneck exterior. Marcus sported a jeans outfit that did nothing at all to hide his rock-hard body. Monte had a body on him; that went without saying. But little bro's body was ripped to perfection. This type of body was not typical of the men I had seen; not even Dante's body looked like that. A couple of years in lockup had done this young boy's body some good. Marcus lacked the polish of his big brother, but Lord knows, he made up for it in other areas that I could only imagine.

Back to reality, Nina, I told myself. He was without a doubt off-limits in more ways than one.

I greeted Marcus and then showed him the way to

the kitchen and introduced him to Nikki for the second time. They hugged like they were old friends, and Nikki casually offered Marcus a drink.

"Ahh, no thanks," he stated. "I'm not much of a drinking man myself, but I tell you what. If Ms. Nina doesn't mind, I wouldn't mind sparkin' the ism with you two ladies."

Marcus proceeded to pull out a blunt and a lighter, raising his eyebrows for permission to light up. Nikki and I shared a look. I knew this was right up her alley, and even though getting high wasn't my thang, I gave the green light.

I guess I never really understood the thing about weed smoking. I tried it a few times growing up. There always seemed to be a healthy supply of paper joints scattered in ashtrays about our apartment. My momma did little to hide her vices, and we had better not fix our mouths to comment on them, either.

Maybe I didn't know what I was doing or didn't inhale. All I knew was I usually ended up tripping off of everybody around me trippin'.

Marcus took the first hit and passed it on to Nikki, who wrapped her lips around it like an old pro, took a puff, and then passed it back to Marcus.

"So, Nikki, you shot a brother down pretty quick that night at the club. What did I do to deserve that?" Marcus asked in between puffs. He did a final puff-puff before he passed the blunt.

Nikki hit the blunt and then let the smoke flow casually out of her sexy lips, maintaining eye contact with Marcus all the while. She sipped her drink and took another hit, still looking Marcus in the eyes, as if she was sizing up what he was made of, testing his very manhood.

Marcus leaned casually in my kitchen chair, mustering up the best nonchalant look he could manage. All the while realizing that he was playing a hormone-infused game of chicken, he waited for Nikki to make the next move.

"You wanna keep crying over spilled milk, or are you going to step up to the plate while you got the bat?" Nikki commented as she took another sip of her drink.

"Yeah, hell yeah, I'm gon' make my move. I was just saying—," Marcus explained until Nikki cut him off.

"Strike one," she said, with a grin. Getting up from the table, Nikki took a good hit of the blunt and leaned over Marcus, pressing her lips against his.

Marcus opened his mouth to receive her offering and was rewarded with a light kiss. Nikki's back was toward me, and all I could view of the scene playing out before me was Nikki's thick hips posted against the table. She had her drink and the blunt in the other.

"Stand up. Let me see what you're working with," Nikki commanded.

Marcus stood at attention. Slowly and methodically, Nikki sat her drink to the side and passed the philly to Marcus. As she moved to his zipper, his eyes opened wide.

This is about to get good, I told myself, taking a gulp of my drink. I felt like an apprentice watching the master go to work.

Nikki slid her hand into Marcus's pants and stroked his goods carefully. "You like that, don't you?" she said. It was a statement really. No need for Marcus to answer, but he did, anyway.

"Yeah, I like it a lot. What else you got for me?"

Marcus looked like a kid in a candy store. Hell, so did I, for that matter.

Nikki didn't bother to answer the man; she just continued her exploration. I could see her lean forward and tighten her grip on Marcus's manhood. "You know I dig a nice set of nuts, don't you?" she said. Again, it was not a question, but nevertheless, he answered.

"Didn't know it before, but I definitely know it now."

Marcus was holding his breath; he was so damn scared he might say the wrong thing and make it to strike two.

"Follow me," Nikki said simply as her hips danced methodically out of the room. She disappeared down the corridor leading to the steps to my bedroom. Marcus followed like a snake under the spell of an expert charmer. He was definitely caught up in the rapture. It took only a second for him to stumble his ass back into the kitchen, with a boyish grin on his face.

He lifted the blunt in his hand and muttered, "My fault. I forgot about this, Ms. Nina," as he handed it to me and bolted out of the room.

I looked down at the blunt. *Well, hell,* I thought to myself. Marcus had gotten more than he'd bargained for and then some. Now shit.

I sipped on my drink and took a couple of good hits to see if I could get a taste of this "getting high" thing. I closed my eyes for a second, trying to relax into my buzz, all the while imagining what could possibly be going on upstairs. Curiosity was getting the best of me, but low and behold, my girl did not disappoint me. The next thing I knew, Nikki was peeking around the corner, exposing her pretty face and delicate shoulder line.

"Hey, ain't no harm in you enjoying the view. Make me another drink, and meet us upstairs."

As usual, whenever Nikki's bossy ass spoke, it was a command. But on this occasion, I had no problem following orders.

I have to admit I was a little bit salty when they left the room, because I wanted to see the scene unfold right there on the kitchen table. Now that would have been some shit.

I quickly made two more drinks and headed up the stairs, fully enjoying my buzz by now. I think the smoking weed thing had gotten the best of me.

I walked into the room to see both Nikki's and Marcus's bodies showing brightly in the light of the television. The Spice Channel was on the tube, and the sights and sounds of sex only enhanced the scene.

Marcus was just leaning down to pull Nikki's thong off of her thick, creamy thighs, and as he rose to tug it off her body, I couldn't help but notice the rock-hard erection he was packin'.

Damn, baby brother had gotten all the goods! Monte must have learned to get his munch game on point early in life. Growing up with all that dick standing next to him when taking a piss had to do something to a big brother's ego.

Marcus went straight for the goods, pausing only for a moment to admire Nikki's youthful breasts before he bent to kiss them. I could see Nikki's back arch into his lips as he trailed a path from one magnificent breast to the other. Marcus was impatient and rock hard as he tried to move quickly through the foreplay and get to the business at hand.

He trailed a path of kisses down the length of Nikki's small frame, grabbing a handful of hips so he could lick and nip at her ass. She purred with pleasure but cut him short when he braced himself on one arm and prepared to dive into her.

"Strike two, Marcus. You missed a spot," she told him.

Now shit, I thought to myself. I liked a bitch telling a brotha what she expected.

Marcus looked like he couldn't comprehend what she was telling him, so she showed him to the light. Rising on her elbows and looking him in the face, she spread her legs and nodded her head down south. "You know what to do. Taste it, baby boy. Trust me, it's sweet." She rested her head back on the bed and waited for him to comply.

I sat Nikki's drink on the dresser and slid into a corner by the bedroom door, waiting to see Marcus make the next move. Slowly and hesitantly, he fumbled around like he was sizing up his meal. Unlike his big bro, a pussy eater he was not.

Marcus licked carefully, as if he was testing the waters, placing small kisses around her hips and thighs. Nikki had no problem teaching the boy what to do. "You scared of a little pussy, Marcus? Go ahead. Put your face in it," Nikki said.

Step by step she coaxed him to where she needed to be. "Smell that clean, sweet pussy? That's some good, sweet pussy. Taste it." Nikki didn't give the boy any time to decide; she raised her hips to his chin, and the rest was history. Nikki had handed Marcus the pussy on a platter. Now, Marcus might not have been a pro, but his soft, hesitant licks turned into the eager licks and sucks of a pupil that was determined to please his teacher.

Nikki ground her thick hips into his face, and he lapped up her offerings. I was not sure if he was trying to get it over with or if he had chosen to give in and was aiming to please. Either way, seeing this young'n, who was obviously new to pussy eating, go to town was turning me on.

"Lick that sweet pussy. That's some good shit, ain't it?" Nikki asked.

This time it was a question, and Marcus replied with a mouthful of pussy. "Uh-huh."

"I knew that was right," I thought to myself. That was just what I needed to see to get the little knob between my legs throbbing. I licked my fingers and put my drink to the side. Wrapping two fingers around my clit, I slid the other hand down farther and stuck two more into my syrupy, wet pussy, which had gotten that way from the sheer pleasure of engaging in voyeurism. I began tickling my G-spot with one hand and teasing my clit with the other while I watched the couple before me.

Marcus finally decided to take control of the situation like the roughneck that he was. He raised himself up so that he was towering over Nikki's small frame. The nigga wiped his face off like he had finished a bucket of chicken only to realize there weren't any napkins in sight.

Grabbing his dick, he looked at Nikki like she was going to pay for making him eat pussy. Nikki looked back at him, as if to say, "Nigga, what?" and it was on. Marcus tossed Nikki's thick ass legs over his shoulders and slowly slid that fat dick into her pussy.

Nikki raised her hips to meet him and then slowly

but surely took in all of that nice, hard dick, like a champ.

"That's my girl," I said, still working on my own nut.

I watched them with my eyes half shut, imagining what it would be like to join in on the fun. Once Marcus opened Nikki's pussy up, he began to grind in the pussy like he was slow dancing. I could see the muscles in his back and ass moving up and down like he was a fucking wild animal.

"Damn, little bro! How can I be down?" I said to myself, with a moan, imagining that it was his dick inside of me and not my own fingers.

Nikki was working her pussy from underneath. Bracing herself on the balls of her small feet, she raised her hips to meet every thrust Marcus threw her way. The sounds of wetness filled the air. Nikki's pussy was talking to him, and the sound of it made me want a ten-inch dick of my own.

As usual, Nikki regained control of the situation. Pushing Marcus up, she tossed her leg over and let him hit it from the side. It must have been too much dick from that angle, because Marcus had the best of her for a minute.

Grabbing the circumference of her waist, he worked her out, and I knew that big pipe was in her guts. After about ten strokes, she got a hold of herself and raised herself onto her knees. Faced with a mountain of ass, Marcus looked shocked and amazed as she started to drop that ass on him. The nigga looked like a rag doll, arms out at the side, getting tossed around my Nikki's buxom ass.

Nikki fucked him like she was about to get paid for it. Rising up on her small feet, she brought Marcus to a kneeling position and continued her assault on his pipe. She was enjoying this, and so was I. My own moans began to fill the air, and I stroked my pussy in earnest, trying my best to reach fulfillment.

In the midst of my masturbation, I realized that Nikki was trying her best to bring Marcus to his knees. A sadistic smile curled her sexy lips into a snarl, and she smacked her fat ass cheeks on the boy's pelvis like she was seriously trying to break him off.

Marcus regained control and flipped the script. With one good buck, Nikki dropped to her stomach, and Marcus was right behind her. Lifting her healthy leg up, he tossed her back onto her side and gave it to her hard. The sound of Nikki's wetness only served to turn us both on, and Marcus popped his hips in and out of her sloppy wetness like a pro.

All we needed was the porn music, because a real live porno was going down right before my eyes.

Turning so she could look him in the eyes, Nikki had a look on her face like she was pissed she had been overcome. "Don't start nothing you can't finish," she said. She gave the nigga a heads-up before she went on to demand, "You hear me? Don't start nothing you can't finish. Keep it up. Keep it up!" She was challenging him, and despite the angle that he was hitting it from and the size of his dick, she looked him in the eyes and gyrated her hips with all her might.

My fingers were about to fall off, I was going at it so hard. "Umm," I moaned as I felt my nut coming on strong. "Oh yeah. Here it comes . . . Here it comes."

Just as I was about to explode, I dug my fingers deep in my pussy. I removed one wet hand from my clit and assisted my other hand in reaching my orgasm. Fuck! Looking at Marcus's shiny, wet dick wreak havoc on Nikki's pussy took me over the edge. "UMMM . . . there it is! Oh yeah! Oh yeah!"

My orgasm must have broken Marcus's concentration, because when he took one look in my direction, his façade crumbled into two. His lip quivered like he was trying to man up, but there was to be no such luck.

Right before he came, Marcus looked like he was about to burst into tears. "Uh . . . huh . . . uh . . . huh," said Nikki, coaxing him into coming despite himself. She wasn't a good sport about him nuttin' before her, either. "Strike three. Game over," she whispered.

"It ain't over yet. Gimme a minute," Marcus pleaded, gasping for air.

Poor baby. He tried his best not to go out like a punk. Hey, in my book, he got an A+, but I wasn't his teacher.

Nikki didn't even take a second to lay up. She rolled off the bed and walked proudly over to the dresser to retrieve her drink. "That was good, huh?" she asked me simply, like I wasn't a pile of mush my damn self.

She stepped over me and proceeded into the bathroom, leaving Marcus and me in a bit of an uncomfortable situation. With no third party in the room, the scene became a little uncomfortable. I shook off the feeling, though. The way I saw it, he was in my damn house. Let him be the one shook up.

I rose to my feet and adjusted my clothes. Picking up my drink to finish it off, I allowed my eyes to feast on the chiseled frame that lay on my bed. Pausing on the sight of his swollen pipe, I couldn't help but notice that despite its softness, that joker was still on point.

My eyes flew to his face, realizing I had spent too much time admiring the view. Marcus looked me in the eyes, with a grin on his young face. "You can have some, too," was all he said.

Umm. The tone of his voice and the look in his eyes gave me a tingle. "You're not telling me nothing I don't know, young'n," was all I had to say to that. I turned to leave and then added, "Get dressed before you get too comfortable."

As I proceeded to the living room, where I could lie down and relish my buzz, I closed my eyes so I could replay the sight of Nikki and Marcus's soiree. I wanted to record each detail in my brain before I got too tipsy to remember the details.

It wasn't long before a refreshed Nikki, smelling like she had removed all traces of Marcus from her person, and a suddenly shy Marcus came to join me in the living room. Marcus had the nerve to look bashful. I couldn't comprehend if that look was because of his not-so-subtle offer to me, or because I had been a witness to the beating his dick had just taken from my girl's pussy.

They stood at my front door, shit talking and exchanging info, before they both turned to me to say their good-byes. Marcus resorted to a humble "Take care, Ms. Nina."

I'm not sure how I earned the Ms. in front of Nina, especially at this point in the game, but I acknowledged him with a nod and said, "Good night, Marcus. Be safe."

As soon as the door closed behind him, Nikki

turned to me, with a grin on her face, and confessed, "Girl, I needed that!"

Nikki and her old man had been going through the ringer, and in my opinion, tonight had been an easy fuck with a boy toy that she could manage. Besides that, it might have also been a little bit of get back for her dude's past indiscretions in their relationship.

"Well, I hope you got your mind right," I replied to her.

"Oh, girl without a doubt." With a wink and a hug, she was out the door, calling out, "I'll call you tomorrow. Let's do lunch!"

I locked the door behind her and did a quick check to make sure the house was secure. Heading into my bedroom, I thought about changing my sheets for a split second and decided that keeping them on would only aid me in busting for a second time tonight. I reached in my armoire, glanced at my vibrators, and decided to grab the biggest one in my possession. Lying in the middle of my bed, I closed my eyes and revved up my big boy. Now it was time for me to get my mind right.

Chapter Twelve

It's Getting' Hot in Here

Lying on Dante's chest listening to the raspy voice of Lauren Hill sing "Sweetest Thing" made me wish this moment could last forever. Gliding my fingertips across the plains of his smooth skin I listened to her words and allowed myself to relish in the moment. "The sweetest thing I've ever known. Was like the kiss on the collarbone." Lauren sang and I concurred. *Tell me about it girl*, I thought to myself. The past week had been heaven on earth, with Bridget out of town attending a forensic accounting seminar, whatever the fuck that was. I enjoyed carefree days and steamy nights with Dante all to myself. This was the first time we had got it on in his apartment without it being a quicky. We took our time, meeting each other here after the gym. He cooked while we talked shit and laughed over a bottle of wine.

Inwardly I had to chuckle to myself thinking of the dismay my time spent with Dante had caused

Monica. She was not a happy camper. I understood my girl's position, or at least I tried to, but, lying in Dante's arms I didn't have a care in the world. Monica left me a message Monday night commenting on the fact that we were both noticeably absent from bowling and she had to cover for me by saying I was sick. I didn't ask Monica to take such precautions. She was dealing with her own guilt. I decided that was Monica's problem not mine.

Monte was another issue, he was getting a little beside himself. We had some good times together but, I was sure he had another piece of tail on the side. The confusing thing about it is now that I wasn't available anytime he called, he was starting to trip. For instance, three nights ago, he showed up unannounced and, needless to say, I was pissed. Myles and Ariel stood behind me at the door looking at this fool, him looking back at us.

"You gonna let me in?" Monte had the audacity to ask like he was paying bills.

"Nope" I replied. Monte looked dumbfounded. I put one hand on my hip and looked him up and down like "now what nigga?"

He bowed out gracefully, with just a bit of attitude, "Enuf said, I ain't the one to disrespect your shorties Nina, but I was concerned. I mean, you barely even hollered at a nigga, you know what I'm sayin'?" He continued "I was tryin' my best to show you a few things, be good to you, is this how you repay me?"

I had the nerve to feel sorry for him for half a second. That is until he spoke that last sentence. I smacked myself back to reality. Reality being, Dante was coming over and I had to get this nigga off my porch and put these kids to bed, so with that in mind I made it short and sweet.

"Look Monte, if you can't understand that I am a single mother with two children and a full time job, then I don't know what to tell you. Really Mo, I'm not some project chick sitting around waiting for you to take care of me." I stepped out on the porch long enough to get my point across without the kids lapping up everything I said.

"One more thing, Monte, let me set something straight for the record. While I've appreciated the gifts, the trips, and every thing in between, those are just extras, don't get it twisted, I'm not for sale. The little things you've done for me don't pay the mortgage, car note, or any mother fuckin' bills in this bitch, so the next time you feel like your extras qualify you to stop by my crib without checking in first, think again." Before he could respond I turned and stepped back in the house gestured to my babies and said "As you can see, this is a bad time for me. I'll call you." With that said I gave Monte the heads up and shut the door. He watched me until the door was shut in his face. Monte was sporting a puppy dog look. I didn't care, he was just something to do.

Pushing thoughts of Monica and Monte aside I decided to focus on the present. Knowing our time spent together was limited I intended to take full advantage of the situation. We had just had a marathon sex session, if it wasn't for our training sessions I might have punked out in the first round.

"A girl could get used to this good lovin' ya know?" I had said.

"Right, my thoughts exactly. What am I gonna do when you get a man?" Dante continued, "I'm a stingy man. I don't think I could share." Dante chuckled, but he was the only one laughing. I hated when he fronted like there wasn't any real chemistry between us.

"You know, you could have me all to yourself, if you manned up." I could feel myself getting caught up in my emotions and I tried to reign in the feeling that was making my chest want to explode. I looked Dante in the face to try and read his expression. He smiled, I melted.

"Nina, baby, you know you're my baby, right? Gimme a kiss." He was bullshitin' me and I knew it. But I kissed him, and felt the butterflies spring to life in my stomach. "We're always going to be the coolest, I promise you that. Besides, you got too much going on for a low maintenance man like myself."

Before I could protest, Dante's phone rang. It was his bitch, I could tell by the ring tone that was reserved for her. I rolled out of Dante's arms and copped an attitude on the other side of the bed. It bothered me to no end to have to play my position as the chic on the side. I tuned in to what Bridget had to say, hoping she would keep it short and sweet. It wasn't long before I noticed Dante's relaxed tone quickly changed to an anxious stutter.

"Damn baby, why didn't you tell me you were coming home today, I would have had something planned for us. You at the airport, now?" I looked back at Dante to see him shooting me a distraught look. I rolled over, raised one eyebrow and smiled back at him. Now what playa, I thought to myself. I didn't have long to wander.

"Right, okay baby. Okay, I'll see you in a minute. I love you, too." Dante slammed his phone shut.

"Shit Nina, she's on her way! Fuck! She's on to us

I can tell. It's that female bullshit she's trying to pull!" Dante was pissed, I'd never seen him like this.

"How do you figure?" I was curious where he was going with this.

"You know Monica dropped dime on us. Come on baby girl, I hate to rush you, but I gotta get this place together." Dante rushed around the apartment, tossing my clothes, throwing the covers on the bed. Oh hell no, he was putting my black ass out! I was salty, pissed and some other indescribable shit. I stomped around the apartment gathering the pieces of clothing he had missed.

Dante rushed out the bathroom, drying off his dick and leaned in to kiss me. "Spare me, really, don't half-ass try to make the shit all right, okay?" I skipped around the room on one foot trying to lace up my sneaker.

"Come on, Nina, baby, work with me here. You knew what was up, fuck! Female shit!" Dante continued rumbling while he haphazardly tried to get his place in order. I jerked the last of my belongings into my gym bag, tossed on my jacket and headed for the door.

"I'm outta here, pimp. Talk at you later." I yelled over my shoulder.

"Hold up! Baby, you can't go out the front door, she might pull up!" Dante was a wreck, but I was in no mood to play my fuckin' position, not this time.

"What the fuck are you insinuating Dante?" I rolled my neck and gave him the look, you know which one I'm talking about.

"Nina, could you please go out the back door? Please, baby, come on now Nina." He was desperate, I wanted him to suffer. I took a second to access the situation and headed to the back door. Monica would have my head and that's about the only reason I threw in the towel gracefully.

"Thank you for understanding baby. I'll make it up to you, promise." Before I could respond he continued, "Oh and baby, can you look for headlights before you go to your car, she could be pulling up any minute now."

I stopped dead in my tracks and raised my hand just enough to let Dante know he had gone too far. Turning to face him I planted a look on my face that should have burned the nigga.

"Dante, remember this, Bridget's your bitch, not mine, okay? You fuckin' watch for the bitch's headlights and if you see them and you still see me, well then you know you got some explaining to do, huh playa?" I threw open the door and stepped outside while Dante was trippin over his words.

"Nina, baby, you know I would never play you. Work with a brother, would you?" This man was my Achilles heel, I knew it the moment I stepped out that back door so he could save face.

"Trust me, I am working with you the best I can considering the fact that I was the one comin' less than a half hour ago." I gave him a peck for good measure. "Have fun explaining the reason your dick ain't happy to see her. I'd pay cash money to be a fly on the wall for that one."

Dante's eyebrow's flew up at the realization that I had drained him. I turned to head around the side of the apartment building and added, "Don't forget about the wine glasses, baby!"

"Oh shit!" I heard Dante exclaim. For the moment, I was satisfied that I had sent him into a tailspin for making me play bottom bitch.

Chapter Thirteen

If I Was Your Girlfriend

The sun was just beginning to peek over the rooftops, giving the false hope that there actually might be some warmth on this cold winter morning. I lay in my bed, with pillows surrounding me; I was trying desperately to give myself a false sense of security. For the first time in my life, I had made an attempt to let my hair down, to live for me. Not for my mom, my sisters, my brothers, my children, my husband, my job. I was just going to live for Nina.

Well, needless to say, I had gotten myself into a pretty fine mess. So here I lay, starring at my motionless ceiling fan as if it were going to spring to life, smack me in the face, and give me some direction.

Two things were for certain: Number one, if I didn't seriously slow my roll, I was going to end up with more miles on my pussy than the old-school Cadillac my grandpa kept in the garage. Number two, my babies needed their momma here at home, the mother they were used to waking up to every day of their natural lives. I was that mother who had been at every event, from preschool graduation to breakfast with mom.

I was feeling myself, and in my whirlwind of self-centered attention, for lack of a better word, I had neglected my babies. They were too young to ever understand, but they gave me my strength in my darkest hour. After my husband left me and I was on the verge of what felt like death, seeing their little faces made me straighten up, put my shoulders back and my chin up, and keep it moving. Last but not least, if I didn't regain my focus, I was going to lose my footing at work, and I couldn't afford to let that happen. I had worked too hard to gain my position. But lately, my late nights on a mission to fulfill my list of fantasies seemed to have taken priority over everything else. But looking up at my wall calendar, I realized that there were only a couple more weeks in February, and after I accomplished my mission, things could return to normal . . . couldn't they?

But how would I recover? How would I make amends? And most of all, how would I appear to not give a fuck about the folks who had my name on their lips . . . or my pussy?

I made a mental note to self to look at the folks who had opinions about how I was living and say, "Fuck you!" For the most part, people with opinions are stupid fucks, so let them have at it. I had enough on my plate to worry about what other people thought of me. As far as I was concerned, I deserved to be free after an eight-year prison sentence of marriage to that rat bastard.

Just when I had convinced myself that what other

people said about me didn't matter, I got the ultimate smack in the face. Monica called me up one day, saying that she needed to talk to me. I couldn't imagine what it was that she needed to talk to me about. I must admit, though, I had been in my own little world. I had been lucky enough to make a turn that wasn't on MapQuest and land my hot ass right in Erotic City. But as I toured the quaint little town, I seemed to have failed to keep in touch with my BFF like I had done in the past.

Trying my best to support a friend in need, per Monica's request, I showed up at her apartment after work to find her sitting on her couch, looking at the floor, with a pensive look on her face.

Monica, the consummate party girl, had never looked this down before. I felt bad that my girl had been dealing with some shit and I was none the wiser because I'd been too busy being fucking Tom Cruise on a mission impossible.

I decided to try to cheer her up, so I came right in, sat down next to her, and put my arm around her. "What's up, Momma? Who did it? Let me at 'em," I said in an effort to lighten the mood. "Tell me who did it to the baby."

Monica chuckled softly and turned her head, as if she couldn't bear to speak the words to me, much less look at me. "You did, Nina," Monica said matter-of-factly. "You did it."

I was stunned by her comment, and my face had the confusion I was feeling in my heart written all over it. I searched her eyes and facial expression for a sign that she might be joking, but she was dead serious.

Monica continued. "You did. The way you've been

acting lately, that's what's got me feeling the way I'm feeling now, which isn't too good, Nina."

"What did I do?" I honestly hadn't a clue what I could have possibly said or done to have my girl feeling salty about me. But she filled me in on my ignorance soon enough.

"You got divorced, and it just completely changed your steelo. I mean, you're the bomb and all, and nobody can take that away from you, but maybe you never realized that you have always been the bomb. You were the bomb before the divorce, boo." Monica paused momentarily.

"Look, Monica, I'm sorry if the fact that I'm just stepping up my game in life has you trippin', but—"

Monica cut me off. "I'm just sitting here trying to figure out since when stepping up your game included fucking in our circle."

"The circle?" My mind was spinning. How in the hell did I become the villain? Before I could wrap my lips around a response, Monica continued her assault.

"Let me break it down further. I know about you and Dante and y'all's little solo act, but dammit Nina, the man is engaged!" Monica threw her hands up as if she didn't even want to hear a response to the question she had posed. "Look, that doesn't even matter. What does matter, Nina, is that your ass isn't your only asset, but I'm not sure you know that, so I'm here to remind you that you don't need to stick your ass out every time we take a fucking picture or be the first one to make yourself known whenever a fine brother walks in the room. Your attitude has changed, and whenever the old Nina decides to resurface, my home girl, my main bitch, my ride or die chick, hey,

I'll be there for her. But right now, we need to give each other some breathing room because I don't know you anymore, baby, and at the rate you are going, I don't know if I want to."

Where was this shit coming from? This shit that was fucking cutting my heart like a knife. Monica, my BFF, had Michael Meyersed me, and now I was sitting there, bleeding all sorts of emotions on her nice furniture. This was not happening to me. This could not be happening to me, and of all people, how could it be Monica spittin' the venom?

Perhaps I should have tried to put myself in Monica's shoes and see where she was coming from regarding the situation. Perhaps the old me would have. But I said, "Fuck that shit." If a mutherfucka shoots at me first, I shoot back, and I shoot to kill. Besides, since when did Monica become a poster child for living righteously? How in the fuck did she even fix her mouth to form the words about how I was getting down when she had been right up in the mix when Dante and I started screwing? Hell, Monica had pretty much set this ball in motion, and now that this snowball had grown into an avalanche, she wanted to toss me to the wolves. It was like she was jealous or some shit, like she wanted to fuck him. Well, I'll be damned. So even though my insides were burning with heated flames, I allowed my words to be cool as they slipped off my lips.

"You made some valid points," I told her, "and by all means, I'll take that into consideration, but I have a few things of my own that I need to say. So let me set a few things straight." I moved from my spot on the couch, because it was apparent I was the one needing some direction. "Since when does my ride or die chick do me a fucking favor by giving me some space because I made a bad call? How dare you fix your mouth to judge me when you been fucking indiscriminately for the past six years! How many men would need to be swabbed if you popped up pregnant, Monica?"

"Now hold up, Nina," Monica interrupted, but the damage was done. I had let her say her piece; now it was my turn.

"Ain't no hold up, Monica. You're wrong. You're wrong, and for once you aren't being truthful about how you live, because your guilt got ahead of you, and instead of accepting it, you placed your damn guilt on my shoulders. It's cool, though. Here is what I'm going to do. I'm going to give you a chance to marinate on what just went down, what part you played in it. And last but not least, how you want to spend the rest of our friendship. So on that note, peace." I gave her the two fingers, the peace sign, grabbed my coat, and headed for the door.

Monica called my name as I headed out the door. The cold didn't even phase me, I was so pissed. How was she going to play me for a bitch that was a friend of a friend? Hell, she acted like I had fucked her damn man. I was pissed, but I was also hurt. I jumped in my truck and headed toward home, barely holding on to my tears. Monica had never judged me, or I her, and yet here we were, at odds over dick and pussy.

That was three days ago. I got a voice mail from Monica saying we were better than this and needed to talk. Talking was not something I was prepared to do until I got my mind right, so once again, here I lay, looking at the ceiling fan, then over at the wall calendar, contemplating my next move.

Chapter Fourteen

Time Out

The sweet smell of homemade cookies filled the house, and the constant beeping coming from the oven alerted us to go check on our sweet creations. Ariel was running with all of her might to beat her big brother to the finish line. She wanted to be the first one at the stove to help Mommy remove the tasty delights. No sooner had she made it from the TV room, where we had all been lounging while watching a DVD, than Miles zoomed past her, knocking her out of the way as he made his way to the kitchen.

"Nooo . . . Miles! It's my turn. Stop, Miles!" Ariel screamed at the top of her lungs. It hadn't taken long for Ariel to realize she was fighting a losing battle when it came to getting those baked goodies out of the oven, so like any typical four-year-old, she changed her tactics.

Stopping in her tracks and dropping to the floor

in the middle of the hallway, she reached back to her terrible twos and threw a full-blown temper tantrum. Arms and legs flying, she screamed as if the house was on fire and she was calling out to be rescued. "Mommeee! Miles got to get the cookies the last time!"

I couldn't help but chuckle as I stood in the doorway of the TV room. Although it was a wonderful effort on my little girl's part, Ariel's tactics worked much better on her dad than on me. Besides, this wasn't what I had in mind when I designated today as Mommy's time with the babies.

It was no secret, I needed some time out with my babies, and it was evident in their little faces that the children truly needed this time with me. It was even more evident in Ariel's behavior that the lack of Mommy and babies' time was starting to affect her. I could read right through her tantrum. It derived less from defeat against her brother and more from a desire for attention, my attention.

I headed for the kitchen, and without breaking stride, I scooped Ariel up from off the floor and right into my arms. "Calm down, little girl. Hissy fits are not ladylike," I reminded her.

When I carried my red-faced baby girl into the kitchen, we were greeted by the delighted grin of six-year-old Miles. My little man was standing by the oven, with his chest poking out. He was clearly showing off the fact that he had won once again.

His display of victory sent Ariel back into a frenzy. She straightened her body, threw up her little arms, and exclaimed, "Mommy! Miles is teasing! He's teasing me, Mommeee!"

What had elicited a slight chuckle from me at first

was now just over-the-top dramatics, and I had completely had it with the tantrums. I released her from my arms. The minute her little feet hit the floor, I dropped to my knees, put my hands on Ariel's tiny shoulders, and gave her a small squeeze to get her attention.

"Ariel Elizabeth, cut it out right now!" I said. Being the drama queen that she was, Ariel continued whimpering and squeezing out tears that didn't really want to come out but eventually did, owing to her persistent ways.

I could clearly see that divorce and my current lifestyle had taken quite a toll on my innocent babies. I knew that one day of baking cookies wasn't going to fix things. But it was a start, a start that I knew I had to finish. It wasn't just about Ariel and her fits. Little Miles, who was typically rambunctious and outgoing, was much more reserved now.

Ariel had always been bossy by nature, but now she had upped the ante on her bossy ways by becoming very opinionated and demanding. Their father had noticed this in her as well. We both agreed that the children's having to get acquainted with two households was definitely sending them into a tailspin. Ariel's temper tantrums had increased tenfold, and although her daddy became putty in her hands each time she threw a fit, I was in no mood to accommodate her tantrums.

"Ariel's a little baby," Miles interjected. He stood at the stove, poking his tongue out, taunting his sister, with a thumb in each ear while he wagged his fingers.

"I'm not a little baby, Miles!" Ariel yelled over my shoulder as if I wasn't right there in front of her.

I put my two cents in. "Well, if you're not a baby, stop acting like one," I said, moving my face so that it was smack in front of hers, keeping her brother out of her sight. "Fits are for babies that have no control, Ari, and you are Mommy's big girl. You're not a little baby like Haliegh, are you?" I asked, reminding her of the newborn baby my ex sister-in-law had just given birth to.

"I am Mommy's big girl," she responded with authority, wiping her tears away. Ariel's pride had kicked into full gear. She straightened her small back and lifted her chin pridefully.

"Good girl. Now let's check on the cookies," I said, standing up and heading over to the stove, where Miles was standing.

I turned on the light in the oven and watched as my two children huddled around the glass window, with excitement. Ariel and Miles peeked through the oven window and squealed in unison, "The cookies are done!"

I couldn't help but smile at their delight. I exhaled, relieved that I had gotten the situation back under control. "Now what comes first?" I asked.

"Safety first!" Ariel said, looking very proud of herself for beating Miles to the punch.

"Right. Now hand Mommy the oven mitts, Miles," I ordered.

Miles dutifully handed me the oven mitts. "Oven mitts, check!" Miles stated proudly.

I opened the oven door and took out what was the third batch of cookies we had made that day. This batch was Ariel's favorite: sugar cookies. Miles had gotten first dibs on his favorite, chocolate chip, which were cooling on the baking rack. Miles couldn't keep his little eyes off of them. Turning off the oven and placing the cookie sheet on the stove top to cool, I turned to my anxious children and asked, "How about some lunch while the last of the cookies finish cooling?"

Ariel's facial expression showed that she was down with that. However, Miles had to think about that one, and after doing so, he finally shared his thoughts.

"How about some cookies and then lunch?" Miles said diplomatically. Raising one eyebrow, I gave Miles "the look," and it didn't take but a second for him to comprehend and rethink things through. "Okay, lunch and then cookies," he said pitifully.

Miles and Ariel were sent to wash their hands while I went through the paces of making them a lunch. Taking a quick glance in the fridge, I pulled out carrot sticks and all the fixings to make sandwiches. My roles certainly changed from day to day, and more specifically, from day to night. Especially given my latest nighttime activities.

Thinking back on how my life had changed reminded me of a D. L. Hughley skit in which he yelled out to his kids, "Don't you kiss your mama on the lips!" after she had finished polishing him off. It was funny then, but now as I looked back on it and compared it to my recent sexual encounters, it didn't seem so funny anymore.

Although there was no fear on my part of harming my babies, my conscience tended to sneak up on me and remind me that my social life was anything but motherly.

Every since my first pregnancy was confirmed, I had strived to distance myself from the poor parenting skills of my mother and had tried to be the best little momma I could be. I had delved into all the reading material I could find on prenatal care and childbirth. I had breast-fed both of my little darlings until they were ready to drink from a cup and had cooked homemade baby food to ensure everything that touched their precious lips was all natural. I wondered if my single status and declaration of sexual freedom somehow were at odds with their delicate upbringings. That wasn't something I wanted to deal with. That wasn't something I wanted to face right now. So pushing aside any concern that my children were at risk or that I was a sub-par mother based on my change in lifestyle, I continued with the task at hand.

Finishing up the sandwiches I had been preparing, I grabbed a few cookie cutters we had used a couple of months ago, at Christmas time, and pressed them into the bread, creating a combination of star- and bell-shaped finger sandwiches. As if they were cued, Miles and Ariel came running down the hall and assumed positions at the kitchen table just as I stacked the last sandwich on the serving platter and sat it in the middle of the table. I grabbed three plates from the cabinet and placed two sandwiches on each plate, along with carrot sticks and a splash of ranch dressing on the side for dipping. After I set the plates in front of them, we all settled down to enjoy our afternoon meal.

It didn't take long before Ariel piped up. "Guess what, Mom?" she said with her mouth full of carrots. She wiped ranch dressing from her tiny mouth.

"I'm all outta guesses, Ari. I give up," I replied, picking up a bell-shaped sandwich.

"At Daddy's house, I got a pretty picture on my

bedroom wall. It's really big. Daddy's friend painted it for me. She's pretty." Ariel stopped eating and watched me as she continued describing "Daddy's friend" as if she was painting her very own verbal portrait of the woman. The little rascal seemed to be measuring my reaction.

"Oh really, baby? What kind of picture is it?" I was cool on the outside when I posed my question to the young'n, but inside, I was pissed the fuck off.

I knew that my baby girl didn't mean any harm. She was hurting. She was hurting because Daddy and Mommy weren't together anymore and Mommy didn't seem to be around as much as she used to be.

Rahmel and I had discussed not bringing anyone around the children until the relationship with that person was serious. If Ariel's description was accurate, the "pretty" artist was his Afro model, Malkia, the home-wrecking heifer that the rat bastard cheated on me with in what was the final straw in our marital relationship. Malkia. The bitch's momma had named her Melissa, but I guess that wasn't "black" enough for her, so she made a trip down to the courthouse and got it changed. Malkia . . . Melissa . . . I didn't give a fuck. The only thing that was killing me to know was why he had introduced the whore to my babies. His ass had told me that she meant nothing to him, that what went on between them should never have happened. So someone that meant nothing to him was now playing Picasso on my children's bedroom walls?

Ariel demanded my attention and tore my thoughts away from the rat bastard and his sidekick bitch.

"Mommy? Mommy, are you listening to me?" She bucked her eyes and leaned forward until she was sure she had my full attention. The little diva in training knew that she had inserted the knife. Now it was time to gently turn it. She didn't want to injure me to the point where I bled to death, but like I mentioned before, she did want my attention, and, boy, did she have it.

Acknowledging her with a nod, I urged her to continue her story.

"Well, my wall has a castle with a rainbow and fairies all around. I'm the princess; that's what Daddy says."

Ariel was in her element, so I did my best to appear pleased with the mural her daddy had commissioned his ho to paint on my baby's wall.

Miles chimed in. "She's painting my wall next. I'm getting a racing track around my room, with fast cars racing each other like VRROOOM!"

My children continued to compare portraits while I was dying inside. *This bitch! That ho!* I yelled inside. She was leaving her mark, pissin' on my territory. How dare she!

"Do you know Daddy's friend, Malkia, Mommy?"

Ariel was just like me. She had to get to the bottom of shit. Until she knew that she had pushed just the right button, she was going to keep pressing.

"Yes, baby, we've met," I stated simply, chewing on a carrot as if everything was all right.

"She's nice, huh? I like her hair. Can you do my hair like hers, Mommy?" Ariel inquired, staring me down as if she was working for the enemy.

Again, this was just another tactic Ariel was using to get my attention, but Miles stood up for his momma.

"I like your hair better, Mommy." He shot his sister a look that let her know that she had gone too far.

"Thank you, baby. Now who wants cookies?" I said. I was trying to find a way out of this conversation fast.

"Me!" they sang in unison.

I went over to the stove, and my little helpers were quick to follow. Together, we added sprinkles and icing to our combination of cookies. I let them have at it, and they shoved one cookie into their mouths after another while I collected my thoughts.

This mutherfucker! How could he betray our promise? We had a deal. Hadn't my babies been through enough without introducing a new face into their lives, the face behind the disruption in their lives no less? I was just about hotter than the oven right about now.

Little Ariel had taken to believing that all daddies left sooner or later. I had been embarrassed on more than one occasion by her asking every man that came in contact with her and who had a woman on his arm, "Are you going to leave her like my daddy left my mommy?"

I alerted her dad to the situation. I wanted him to feel it. I wanted him to feel the emotion that was now embedded in our child because of his adulterous actions. Knowing his baby saw him in a less than perfect light stressed him to no end. He had a "talk" with Ariel and assured her that Daddy would never leave her. I hid my smile when she reminded him that she knew he would always be her daddy, but that he did "leave Mommy." Now, that his ass could not dispute.

Ariel was full of anger over her father's and my divorce. She had even resorted to fighting and picking up sticks to display her frustration. Just recently Miles had come flying up the steps to my bedroom, yelling at the top of his lungs. Behind him was Ariel, with a rolling pin in hand, and she was determined to get another lick in before he found refuge. Miles jumped in my arms, with tears rolling down his face.

"Ari hit me really hard," he cried.

Ariel confessed, "Yeah, uh-huh, I did, because Miles pushed me, and you told me that if anybody messes with me, to pick up something and hit them with it."

She was right; I had given her those instructions. I guess we as parents better be careful about the words we speak to our children.

For the first couple of months after Rahmel and I got a divorce, everybody in Ariel's path had to be sure to watch their back whenever Ariel didn't get her way. She might be behind them, aiming to knock their head off their shoulders.

Miles, on the other hand, had assumed the status of man of the house. He had calmed down, and while he had once been all boy, he was now a bit more quiet, and he watched everything, making sure nobody, and I mean nobody, messed with his momma. His grades had dropped dramatically, and he pulled every trick in the book to stay home from school. My babies had certainly been through the ringer, but thinking back on my own crazy childhood, I smiled to myself. They were going to be A-okay. They had no choice; their momma had nothing but the rest of her life to be there and guide them.

With their little faces full of cookies, I made a suggestion. "How about we go outside and make angels in the snow?"

Ariel was all for it, except for one thing. "Can Daddy come over and make an angel, too?" she suggested.

Miles wasn't having it. "Ari! We only make snow angels with Mommy! You know Daddy doesn't make snow angels." He was sticking up for his momma the best he could, and that was all the comfort I needed.

We wrapped up plenty of cookies together, bundled up, and headed outside. You know me by now, though. I put a note on my mental to-do list to check Rahmel's ass about having his ho around my shorties, but for right now, I went racing into my snow gear to see who could make the best snow angel in snow angel history.

Chapter Fifteen

The Confrontation

For some reason, all kinds of shit had been building up inside of me. I guess my little tiff with Monica had just put me in a confrontational mood. For the past three weeks almost, I had been like a playful little sex kitten having a field day with a ball of yarn. Now, all of a sudden, it was time for an intermission in my life. It was time to get a few things in check.

Some of that shit Monica had spit regarding the sudden change in my demeanor rang true. I guess I had been acting like my shit didn't stank, like if I was a man and had a dick, I could suck it my damn self. How did this happen? How did I get to this point in my life? Then it dawned on me. Everything traced back to him; the rat bastard, which only reminded me that I had a bone to pick with his black ass.

It was Friday, his weekend with the kids. This time it wouldn't be a quick drop-off, though. I had some shit I had to get off my chest. It was time I finally confronted Rahmel with all that I had been holding inside of me.

I memorized in my head all the things I needed to say to him. I even practiced a few lines in the mirror, head bobbin', finger pointing, and all. I had every single word I was going to use to shoot his ass down in order, right down to the way I was going to enunciate so that I showered him with spit on occasion.

It was a warm winter afternoon, more like fall than late February. The sun had managed to melt away any traces of the snow from earlier that week. Rahmel and I had arranged to meet at his momma's house, where they were gathering for a birthday celebration. I had called him at about 3:00 p.m that day to arrange the drop-off of the children.

"When I drop the kids off, I need you to come outside for a minute. I want to holler at you for a second," was all I had to say. I could hear his ass exhale, as if to say, "Here we go again."

"Fuck you, dirty dick motherfucker," I thought. *"Bring your ass and keep bringing it until I'm sick and tired of saying my piece. Do your duty, the duty you neglected as a husband, and just keep taking it, because I got eight years of shit to get off my chest".*

When I pulled up in front of his mother's house, it was around 3:15 p.m. "Hey, I'm outside," was all I said before jumping out of my ride to let Miles and Ariel out. "Give Momma some love," I turned to them and said. Wrapping my arms around their small frames, I hugged them both as if my life depended on it.

Could they ever understand that their little faces were imprinted in my head and heart, and that every time I passed them off to their daddy, my heart was splitting into a thousand tiny pieces? Of course, they couldn't. They wouldn't comprehend this level of love until their own seeds were planted. But Miles knew his momma like a book; it was as if his umbilical cord had never been severed.

"Mommy, where's your head at?" he asked after I released him from the hug.

I had to laugh at my little boy for asking me the very same question I had asked him a million times when he seemed to be off in never-never land. I fought my tears back with a vengeance. The smile on my face was bittersweet.

"My head is right here with you, little, big man." I looked into the same eyes I saw every time I looked in the mirror, housed in a perfect brown face. Miles was the spitting image of his mother, housed in a perfect brown body.

"Ma, are you about to cry?" he asked simply.

"Boy, no. Why would I be crying? I have wind in my eyes, Miles. That's all."

Ariel was never one to stand by the wayside. "I'm cold!" she cried. She had interrupted our moment, but it was cool. Whereas Miles was mini me, Ariel looked exactly like her daddy, with an attitude like mine.

Looking at her made me reflect on the phrase I had taught her when she was barely old enough to talk. Folks kept commenting on how she was her daddy's twin, and my selfish ass taught my two-year-old baby a sassy comeback. "I look like my daddy, but my mamma made me fine," she would say, which drove Rahmel absolutely crazy. To hell with what he thought about her smart-ass little mouth; I loved it, and every time I heard the words from her sweet little lips, I smiled inside.

I kissed both of my babies good-bye and told them that Tuesday, the day I was to pick them back up at their daddy's house, couldn't come soon enough. As they ran into their grandma's house to join in the celebration with their cousins and family, I watched Rahmel open the door, give the children a kiss on the forehead, and then proceed to the curbside, where I was casually leaning against my truck.

"Hey, what's going on, Nina?" He sounded impatient, but I couldn't help but notice that his eyes raked over me as if he was trying to remove the layers of clothing I had on. I was sporting a brown bomber jacket with a cream turtleneck underneath and a snug fitting pair of JLO jeans. The brown leather boots with a stacked hooker heel I was sporting added a little umph to the casual hook up.

"Hop in the truck. I need to get this off my chest," I said to him. I walked around the truck and jumped in like I was mounting a horse; I wanted him to know I meant business.

As far as I was concerned, there was no need for pleasantries at this point in the game, so I got right down to business. "I hope you can understand how upset I was to hear that your chick has been making appearances, spending time with my shorties." There it was. That was my beef. Now, nigga, what?

Mel lowered his head. His chin was buried down in his coat for a long time. We both suffered through a moment of silence that went on long enough for me to start feeling disrespected. He had better not fix himself to say that I, the mother of his children, didn't deserve an explanation about what went on in front of the kids. I was liable to get physical with his ass.

When he lifted his head back up, I was given a glimpse of Rahmel that I had rarely ever seen in our marriage. Normally, he was the cool, calm, nonargumentative type, but now I could see a little aggressiveness stirring up in his bones.

"So what's the problem, Nina? You think I need to get permission from you not only on what goes on when I have the kids, but also on what goes on in my household? I left yo' ass, remember? I'm not your husband; I don't answer to you. And besides, they are my goddamn kids, too!"

Oh, so now the thug in this nigga wanted to come out. Ain't that some shit? Okay, I'll admit, I was a little taken aback by his reaction to my concerns. But defeated I was not.

"Whatever, muthafucker," I snapped. I wasn't trying to hear this shit. "You and I had an agreement, or did you forget? But just in case you did, let me enlighten you." I cleared my throat. "We agreed that if we brought anyone we were seeing around the kids, it was only on the grounds of some serious shit, Mel. This shit right here, having that bitch hanging out like it's family time, painting murals on their bedroom walls and shit, it's not cool."

He just sat there, giving me the opportunity to say my piece, so I took advantage of the gap and continued. "What? You settling down with this bitch or something? If not, that bitch ain't got no fucking business around my kids, Mel! Fuck who you want to fuck, but not that bitch, not in my babies' faces. Fuck that. It ain't cool, and you know it! If you're doing this to hurt me, fine, but don't hurt the babies. They know more than you think."

I could feel my blood pressure rising. Yeah, I was pissed off at the rat bastard, but his ho knew exactly what role she was playing in this as well. The fucked-up part about it was that he was allowing her to do it. This nigga was going to make me kill this bitch. I mean, I hated her. She represented every thing I hated in a bitch. She had basically said, "Come on, Rahmel. Leave your family. I got everything you need right here."

Were black women really that desperate for a man that we could look each other in the eye, then stab our sisters in the back?

A friend of a friend had introduced her to us during a Kwanza celebration at our house. I mean, I had actually broken bread with that skank. She came off as all conscience and black power and shit, and she turned around and stabbed her sister in the back. Bitch. Lucky I didn't stab her ass. . . . oh shit . . . that's right . . . I did (different chapter, different book).

Rahmel looked at me as if I were possessed. "Nina, fuck you!" the rat bastard shot back.

If the shock didn't register on my face, let me break it down. Not once in our marriage had Rahmel ever cursed me out. That just wasn't his style. So I knew something else, something other than me checking him about having his woman around my kids, was brewing inside of him. Nonetheless, who the fuck did he think he was talking to? To add insult to injury, though, apparently he wasn't done.

"Fuck you for thinking you can regulate what goes down in my crib when your ass is out here fucking like some dumb-ass project bitch trying to get her rent paid," he shot out of nowhere.

Oh, hell no, he didn't. It was as if I had swallowed a fly. I gulped, trying to figure out where he was coming from with that shit, and to keep my mind from simply wondering, I outright asked him.

"What the fuck are you talking about, Mel? I just started feeling myself, and for the record, I'm way past due when it comes to having a little fun in life. While I was supporting the kids, you were out here fucking like your damn dirty-ass dick was about to fall off, and now you want to check me for moving on? Well, fuck you, Mel! Fuck you!"

I was angry, angry that he of all people was calling me out on my actions. First Monica, and now his ass. This shit was getting hectic up in the truck. And what the fuck did he think he knew about my indiscretions. I knew I had kept my shit on the low, so I couldn't help but wonder who was running their mouth about me.

"You know what, Nina? I can admit to my faults. I can own up to settling down too young because I didn't want to loose my fine-ass pageant chick. I can even own up to not passing up on pussy while we were together, but fuck, Nina, I'm a man. I can choose to not discriminate on the pussy I get. You, on the other hand, might not understand what I know, and what I know is that women don't have the same luxury as men when it comes to fucking. You weren't built to just fuck whoever and walk away. That's what y'all free-for-all fucking asses don't understand. Women can't be like men when it comes to sex. Nina, you can't be like me!"

I swear on everything I love, I wanted to slap the

taste out of his mouth. This nigga was seriously flipping the script on me. This was supposed to be about
the shit that was bothering me. Who did he think he
was, confronting me with the shit he had on his
chest? This was supposed to be my goddamn time.
And besides that, what the hell did he know about
how I had been getting down lately?

While my mind struggled to regain a footing, he
continued to rip me to pieces. "You know what
makes it so bad? The thought crossed my mind to try
and make this thing work between me and you, to get
our family back together, because I realized the im-
portance of family. But now that your name is in
these streets, I can't even see it going down like that."

Did he just slip me the old "You can't change a ho
into a housewife" upper cut? *Okay, bitch. Find your
tongue,* I told myself. I couldn't just let him sit there
and slice me and dice me up.

"What do you mean by that, Mel?" I finally responded. "My name is in the streets because I'm
feeling myself a little bit? I was locked up in the
house, raising kids for years. You barely gave me
enough rope to walk farther than the front porch, and
now that I'm living, or better yet, fucking a little bit,
you want to judge me?"

Mel looked like he wanted to choke the living shit
out of me, but fuck him. Where was he getting this
shit? Was my name really in the streets like that? I refused to believe that a couple of weeks of unadulter-
ated screwing had given me a rep already. That
definitely wasn't my intention.

"I was nothing but true to you throughout our
entire marriage," I told him. "I sacrificed and struggled to get us a little bit of footing, and as soon as I

got it, you left me! Now you want to comfort yourself by putting it back on me, like leading my life led
us to this point."

Mel asked simply, "How many dicks does it take
to please you? How much catching up do you need
to do? Shit, I thought we had a damn good sex life up
until your escapades came to light. Now I'm thinking, 'Damn good thing I left before I embarrassed
myself.'"

This mutherfucker wanted to go for the juggler?
Well, one thing we knew for sure, two could play at
this game. "Nigga, please. You had a good sex life. I
had an Academy Award on my mantle for best actress
in a sex scene, you short dick nigga!"

Oooooh, I knew I was wrong for that, but it was
the truth, and I wanted this nigga to feel me, so I
added insult to injury. "Every time you went to take
a piss after we screwed, I was digging in my pussy,
trying to bust a nut before you came back in the
room. Rahmel, for the record, I would never come
back to your ass, because knowing what coming up
on some real dick is all about has put a whole new
perspective on life, love, and the pursuit of happiness. Cumming equals happiness, and I'm making up
for lost time."

Yes, I thought and patted myself on the back. That
nigga was touched. Salty as a bag of pretzels. But his
ass wasn't going to let me off that easy.

"That's cool. Then what I do in my home don't
even matter. The damage you think I'm causing in
my home by letting old girl chill with the kids can't
possibly compare to the damage you're causing by
generating the same pattern your mother did." His
parting shot killed me softly, only because he knew

I would be thinking about his words for years to come.

The air left my body. Rahmel's words had cut like a knife. I could not believe he went there and was still going. "Lord knows, I'm going to try my best to prevent it," Rahmel said. "But if Ariel ends up putting her goods on the map like you are doing right now, I want you to remember that I warned you to tighten the fuck up."

That apple doesn't fall far from the tree shit went both ways, so I fired back. "First of all, Mel, you can throw low blows all day long, but one that you cannot dispute is the fact that I have been a damn good mother to those children. I've been so good in fact, that your comment about Ariel giving up the goods doesn't phase me at all. What kind of legacy do you think you're laying out for Miles? Is it okay for our son to be out there, fucking like there's no tomorrow, Rahmel?"

Rahmel shrugged his shoulders like it was no big deal. "All in all, Nina, let's keep it real. I'd much rather my son be a ho than my daughter. Whether it's fair or not, men have a fucking permit that women can't have. If you haven't figured that out by now, you will." He ended his comment with a snicker and opened the truck door.

We were both pretty much out of insults at this point. As Rahmel was jumping out of the truck, he turned to give his parting shot. "And another thing. Niggas talk, so tighten up or be prepared to face the consequences." He slammed the door shut, turned around, and walked away without looking back, and for once in a very long time, I was the one left holding the bag. This was some bullshit!

Needless to say, my confrontation with Rahmel hadn't gone exactly as planned. Despite all the evidence of his guilt in the destruction of our marriage, even with all the preparations I had made prior to our encounter, unbeknownst to me, I had come unprepared to plead my own case.

Chapter Sixteen

Making Up Is Hard To Do

I had cut off all communication with Monica. It was killing me. I was about to die the death of a dog. The feeling was almost equivalent to my divorce. I couldn't breathe for thinking about her, but I maintained. I listened to her voice mails.

"Hey, Nina, you know this is some bullshit. Holler at me." I didn't, so she called back. "Dammit, Nina! Call me today. I ain't no nigga, and your pussy ain't good enough for me to be sweating you." She laughed at herself. "Seriously, call me today."

I still didn't. I wasn't ready. My thing was this: right or wrong, my girl was supposed to have my back, ride or die. Now, don't get me wrong. I'm not saying Monica didn't have the right to speak up, because she most certainly did. We'd always been close enough to keep it real and still maintain our love for each other. In my opinion, she just said the wrong things to get her point across, and what was up with that bullshit about "we need some space?"

Fuck that! Monica's defenses were down. She had allowed room for infiltration into our friendship. My main bitch was supposed to maintain her position next to me no matter if we are winning or losing the game.

Having been raised by a family of hustlers I was taught from a young age to believe that there was no room for weakness in your circle. Lord knows, Monica was ace, and even though cutting her off and not accepting her calls was like cutting off my right arm, I maintained my position. The silence was deafening. I was used to an update or two from Monica at least every other day, but her e-mails and voice mails stopped after the first three days. She made one more attempt to get at me, and then nothing. *That's cool, though,* I had thought to myself. We'd just see how things worked out.

Ticktock. Ticktock. Ticktock. I needed my girl back. I got up from my bed and walked over to my dresser to grab me some undergarments to put on after the nice hot shower I was about to engage in, a picture of Monica and I, smiling on the beach caught my attention.

Deep inside, I was also avoiding Monica because she had caused me to put my sex life under a microscope and analyze my actions. But at the same time, she had a lot of nerve. She was as close to a confirmed bachelor as a bachelorette could get. Despite her feminine wiles, Monica carried on like these niggas in the street. Her front door might as well have been revolving, the way she laid up with a brother for a month or three, then conveniently left his shit in a box by the front door as soon as the thrill was gone.

It was a smack in the face to have the consummate party girl put me on the stand and play both judge and jury to my indiscretions. It hurt to have my ace put me in that position. Hell, the way I saw it, I had already been hard enough on myself without any outside help. The fucked-up thing about it was everyone seemed to have something to say about it. I had gotten an earful from Rahmel and Monica about my bad habits. I couldn't win for losing.

I walked over to my bed, sat down, and picked up the phone from my nightstand. I took a deep breath and then dialed Monica's phone number, keeping my fingers crossed that she would answer.

"Hey, you," I said after she picked up on the third ring. The sound of Monica's voice was music to my ears.

"Hey, yourself. Long time no hear from." Monica put the ball back in my court.

"Well, I guess it goes without saying that the longer I stay away from you, the more shit I end up getting myself into. I can admit to having my blinders on, but right now, I just want my girl back." I put my head in the palm of my hand and waited to hear what I knew I had coming to me. No matter what I thought and how I felt, at the end of the day, I had lost my best friend to a life of fucking like there was no tomorrow.

"I missed you, too Nina, and it's fair to say we both said some foul shit the last time we saw each other. I'll own up to my role in putting you and Dante in a

situation that would backfire. The thing is . . ."
Monica was searching for the right words to say.
"The thing is, Nina, this situation has put me in a bad
place with Destiny, Bridget, and you. It's fucked up
to feel like you have to pick a side when you're all
supposed to be playing for the same team."

Monica paused, as if she was allowing me an opportunity to speak. I passed. I had been talking more
shit than a little bit lately. This seemed like the time
to listen.

Monica continued. "You're my girl, always have
been, and I'd never deny you. That would be like
denying myself. I just want to know how you plan on
handling this when we all meet up. Birthday parties,
family celebrations? How do we move on like this
never happened, knowing that what went down is
going to be at the forefront of our minds every time
we're in each other's presence?"

Monica might have been right. Despite the fact
that neither Bridget nor Destiny were close friends of
mine, it would be hard to look Bridget in the eyes
knowing I had been the other woman with no reservations. I had laid down with dogs for too long. Now
I was the one carrying the fleas from one fucked-up
situation to the next. I didn't respect the relationship
Dante had with Bridget, because it interfered with
my desires. In that aspect, I was no different than
Malkia. The shame I felt in that instant of owning
up to the coldhearted, shameless Jezebel I had been
hit me like a ton of bricks.

"Oh, God, Moni, I never intended for it to go like
this, I swear. I just loved the feeling of being with

him. I loved the stolen moments we had together, the jive talking, the reminiscing. I guess it goes without saying, I loved this sex."

I whispered the word *sex* like it was a curse. The good feelings associated with the word had temporarily vanished and had been replaced with an intense feeling of disgust.

"Monica, I can't change what I did. That's a fact. I wish I could rewind the past month and do some things differently, things like not messing up our friendship. The thing about it is, I'm not even so sure the outcome would change. I fucked up. I got caught up. It's okay for you to say 'I told you so,' because you did. Dante was spending so much time 'training' me that Bridget was an afterthought. She didn't even exist in my world. It was just me and him, but now I know better. I should have listened to you. If it's any satisfaction at all, I'm paying the price." I wept silently, allowing the tears to roll down my face unchecked. At this very moment, having my girl back was all that mattered.

"Nina, I would never hope for you to hurt, ever. Not even to satisfy my need for confirmation. I don't have to make you eat your words. Where we come from, you never really learn a lesson unless it's taught to you the hard way." Monica went on. "You remember when we were teenagers and we had both set our sights on Anthony Hawkins?"

I chuckled at the mention of his name. That green-eyed bastard had Monica and me at war. "How could I forget? Remember my aunt striding up to the high school, looking like she was about to set it off when she found out that we were beefin' over a dude?"

I recalled that day like it was yesterday. The

moment Monica and I saw my aunt, we attempted to put our differences about Anthony to the side and run for cover, but it was too late. Aunt Debbie caught up with us.

"I know y'all two-bit heffas see me looking for you! Bring your asses here!" Aunt Debbie was off her rocker just enough that you didn't want to test her, for fear that she would blow a gasket. She looked like she had just escaped from the nuthouse. She used to scare me half to death. The bitch was crazy, God rest her soul, and I knew she was looking down on us, wishing she could smack some sense into our asses now, but what she said that day was true.

"I couldn't believe it when I heard it," Aunt Debbie had scolded Monica and me, "but looking at your shameful faces confirms it to be true. It breaks my heart to think that you would allow some trifling nigga to come between you. You two are as thick as thieves, and he is playing the both of you! You two look desperate, and you're both acting faster than your years! Now what y'all gon' do is squash this mess and pretend it never happened. Ignore that boy like he is the plague!" Aunt Debbie got dead silent and looked back and forth between the two of us like she was daring us to protest.

Neither one of us did, so she continued her rant.

"I want you two to promise never to let no one, man or woman, come between you two. Friends don't let each other down, and they never let the other one suffer, you hear? Years and years from now, I want to see you two sitting together on the porch,

drinking lemonade and knitting blankets. Now
get home!"

Aunt Debbie's lecture was over as soon as it
started. She sent Monica and me on our way, with
our tails between our legs. We did as we were told
and made amends. It wasn't a real falling-out to
begin with. I guess we had both just dug in our nails
more than we both were willing to admit. The cir-
cumstances were different now, but the message remained the same. We were better than that . . . always
would be.

"Monica, I don't know how I'll handle it when I
come face-to-face with Bridget," I told her. "I guess
I'm still working through my feelings on that. As far
as Dante is concerned, we've dropped the private les-
sons. So, needless to say, I no longer have a trainer,
which sucks. I also lost a friend. Before any of this
shit, Dante and I were friends, and now that's no
longer possible. He's dropped me a few e-mails and
text messages over the past week. I e-mailed him
back, but other than that, we haven't hooked up. All
that matters right now is that me and you stay connected. I missed you so much."

I could tell that Monica was crying, because her
voice was breaking up. I decided to try and lighten
the mood. "You know its Ladies Night tonight at the
Grill. You game?" Monica asked.

I hesitated, "I was thinking of something more
along the lines of having a Blockbuster Night. I'm
taking a break from the party scene, the past month
has caught up with my ass light a tsunami," we both
chuckled. "So how about this, me, you, a bottle of
wine and a months worth of drama to catch up on.
Hell, I better make it two bottles of wine."

"Sounds good to me. I'll order the Chinese and turn off the ringers. I want to make sure I don't miss a beat." Monica was back to her old self, and it felt like home once again.

"I got this, Ma," I assured her. "Just be ready for me to stop by in about an hour."

"See you then," Monica said as we ended the call.

I took a deep breath. My call to Monica had gone just the way I'd wanted it to go, if not better. I had gotten back on speaking terms with my BFF, that was the first step in many on my road to making amends.

Epilogue

I, Nina Tracy, promise to tell the truth, the whole truth, and nothing but the truth so help me . . . . *Lord, forgive me . . . dare I say it . . . hell, why not . . .* So help me God.

I might as well call on the Lord now; He is the only one that can save my sinning soul. I got caught up in the power of the p-u-s-s-y. Sex was like a drug, and I was a junkie. Busting became a constant craving for me. Turning out bitches, was a power trip, and I got off on fucking a nigga and leaving him in the dust. By the way, why do men have such a hard time swallowing that pill when bitches give them a taste of their own medicine?

Nonetheless, I loved dishing it out by the spoonful. Knowing I had the antidote to cute a lot of desires made me hungry for more.

Maybe I had buried these craving so deep within me during my marriage that I had created a monster inside of me. A green monster that busted at the seams at the smell of lust in the air and didn't stop to think of the destruction it was causing until the adrenaline had stopped flowing through its veins and the pinnacle of satisfaction had been reached. I did things that I should regret, but don't. And there just might be some things that I have to answer for sooner or later.

No use crying over spilled milk, though what's done is done. So let's talk about it. I did some ho shit, and I liked it. Wait, I take that back. I really liked it. Who am I kidding? I fucking loved it, yo!

I liked the power of demanding attention from men and women. Documenting my escapades in my personal journal and going down the list of fantasies, checking them twice like I was old Saint Nick, seemed easy enough at the time. You best believe I knew who was naughty and who was nice.

Letting an audience in on my bad behavior was a whole different ball game. Nevertheless, I managed to score. Being fresh out on the scene after years of marriage made me a little naive to the game. I thought I was slick enough to keep my bedroom business on the low and still keep up the image that I was as pure as the driven snow. Innocent Nina, the girl that was so warm and sweet that butter would melt in her horny mouth. Well, we all know how that goes. What goes on in the dark will sooner or later come to light.

A wise elder once told me, "You better understand the job before you put on the boots." Suffice it to say, I didn't fully understand the ramifications of my actions, but who really puts forth a lot of thought before they set out on a mission to fulfill their darkest fantasies? Most people don't even have the courage or the guts to put them to paper, let alone seek to fulfill them. Bottom line, despite my experience in other areas, I will own up to the fact that I did some things that I could have very well chalked up to my age—if I was twenty years old. But no such luck. So allow me to own up to for my wanton behavior and to inviting my padres into the pandemonium.

I wanted to play ball and score. I did. I have very few regrets about my explorations. Understanding the power of sexual confidence and the power of pussy gave me a new perspective on life. Now, by no means am I suggesting anybody get their freak on in order to find themselves. It worked for me, but it might not work for everybody else. Of course, there were other factors involved in the metamorphosis that took place after my divorce and changed me into the woman that I am today. Sexual exploration, getting comfortable in my own skin, and letting my hair down were the first steps of many baby steps I took toward rediscovering myself.

The only thing that separates fact from fiction is that the names and places have been changed to protect the not so innocent. We all enjoyed it while it lasted, and we've all since gone our separate ways, with a few exceptions. It goes without saying that my girls ain't going nowhere. We're still as thick as thieves. Monica and I have changed roles since she met and hooked up with Sean Paul, a bona fide nice guy that's hogging up all my girl's time. I'm happy for her, though. She's being treated like a queen and loving it.

After some time, I came to understand the chemistry that makes women and men so different when it comes to sex; women just aren't equipped to lie on their backs with a man and get up with no feelings attached. Not always. Not like men. There are times when exceptions are made. For example, take Monte. I loved being spoiled by him, and his tongue play was on a whole 'nother level, but as far as us becoming an item, it was a no go. He was the typical hustler: money, sex, and bitches were his pursuit, and I wasn't about to become a part of his harem. After our last dinner date, he wanted to fuck, and I wasn't in the mood. He was under the impression that snapping on a six-course meal was equivalent to a golden ticket to enter the Chocolate Factory. I guess it goes without saying that I haven't spoken to him since I kissed him good night and thanked him for the meal. Besides all that, Mel's sister had confirmed that he was the weak link in my armor, running around the city, bragging about the ménage à trois he had had with two bad bitches. Joke's on him, though. Patrice was closer to being my bitch, than his. Both of us decided that if we were going to be outed for eating pussy, it would be by each other. Nothing worse than a gossiping-ass nigga.

On to Dante . . . Damn, that was a tough itch to scratch. How can I put it into words? Dante was my first crush after my divorce. The attention he gave me at the gym and the sex got me twisted. I was wearing rainbow-colored glasses when we were together, not looking at the forest for the trees. We didn't completely severe ties, but I'm proud to say that the last time we happened upon each other in the club, I declined his invitation to do the wild thing in his truck. Two days later, he sent me an e-mail, apologizing for being so forward. But I didn't need his apology. The only person I needed an apology from was myself. I had gone on a mission to please and had gotten caught up in drinking and sex. I had stopped caring for the people that mattered the most to me: my children. I felt like my mother, only worse, because I knew better. But now, I'll spend the rest of my life making up those twenty-eight days to my children.

Dealings with my ex-husband turned baby daddy was a different story. Accepting Malkia as a caretaker and playmate to my children was causing me to seriously consider murder for hire. Despite what I learned from my grimy dealings with Dante, I just couldn't come to terms with Malkia being in the life of my kids. As it turned out, her warranty expired a lot sooner than mine. No sooner had spring turned into summer than Rahmel upgraded, exchanging his African American Barbie for Skipper.

It would take years for Rahmel and me to finally get on common ground and begin speaking again like the friends we were in the beginning. Years of soul-searching led me to realize that I had built the fortress Rahmel had kept me in with my own hands. Searching for a daddy in a man is never the smart thing to do. Maybe if daddies were slightly more available, this epidemic of repeating the cycle would go away. Then again, considering us women live for a man to take the reins and be master of our castles, maybe not. I'm speaking about my own reality, so take what you want and leave the rest.

My brief exploration into sexual fulfillment sent me into a trip that took time and discipline to cure. Sex had become a drug, and even after I came to understand the ramifications of fucking, I found a new form of getting my kicks, via the Internet. As with any addiction, I had to follow a twelve-step program. I went through the motions of discovering the root cause of my fucking with wild abandon. Like most addicts, those steps meant digging into my past and searching for answers. My answers didn't come easy; in fact, it would take years for me to come to terms with the things I had done. But for right now, your twenty-eight days with me are up. Let's talk about it another time . . . different chapter, next book. So until next time, peace.

Love, Nina

About the Author

Nina Tracy is new to the literary industry, with her first published piece of work, *Twenty-Eight Days*, but she's no stranger to weaving exciting, tongue-tantalizing tales. After penning teaser stories, sharing them with her coworkers, friends, and family, and receiving great feedback, Nina knew she had a knack for the written word and, at the same time, had unearthed her passion. A wife and mother of two, this author uses Nina Tracy as her alter ego to freely, and without reservations, share her true life journeys. Nina lives in the Midwest, where she is working on her next novel.